HER FAKE BILLIONAIRE BOYFRIEND

An Overnight Billionaire Bachelor Romance

By Laura Ann

This is a work of fiction. Similarities to real people, places, or events are entirely coincidental.

HER FAKE BILLIONAIRE BOYFRIEND

First edition. May 6, 2019.

Copyright © 2019 Laura Ann.

Written by Laura Ann.

DEDICATION

To the middle sister. Your quick
wit and snarky quips are some
of my favorite things, and often inspire
how I write my characters.
Thank you for putting up with me
for so long!

ACKNOWLEDGEMENTS

No author works alone. Thank you Victorine,
You and your sister make it Christmas every time
I get a new cover. And thank you to my Beta Team.
Truly, your help with my stories is immeasurable.

NEWSLETTER

You can get a FREE book by joining my reading family!
Every week we share stories, sales and good plain fun.
To get in on the action, just visit lauraannbooks.com

PROLOGUE

"I can't decide if we're desperate idiots, or desperate geniuses," Eli Truman grunted as he swung his sledgehammer into the stone wall.

"Does it really matter?" Nelson, his youngest brother said with a laugh. "Either way, we're still here, covered in dust, dirt and who knows what else, renovating an ancient castle." His eyes darted toward the shaking ceiling. "That's going to come down on us at any moment if you don't ease up with the wall toppling."

Eli grunted again, but rested the sledgehammer at his feet.

"You two are the idiots. Everyone knows I'm the brains of this operation," Hayden, the middle brother, said as he hefted an armful of lumber into the space they were working in.

Avangarde castle had become the brothers' last hope. Eli was fresh off a divorce, Hayden had recently gotten fired from his chef job in New York and Nelson had joined because he held no commitment elsewhere. Together, they had pooled their resources and purchased the crumbling structure of bricks they now stood in. The plan was to bring a section of it it up to code and open a bed-and-breakfast.

Nelson rolled his eyes. "Knowing how to make whipped cream doesn't make you a genius."

Hayden glared. "No, but knowing the difference between foie gras and paté might."

"Give it a rest, guys," Eli, ever the diplomat, said as he hefted the sledgehammer again. "After I get this wall down, we can see what we have to work with."

With a loud grunt, he swung at the wall one last time. Dust rained from the ceiling and all three men ducked and covered their heads.

Once they had all stopped coughing, Nelson spoke. "Geez, Eli. Got anger much?"

Eli wiped sweat and dirt from his forehead. "Sorry. That stupid stone has been here for hundreds of years. It doesn't exactly want to come down."

Hayden cocked his head as he stared with narrowed eyes at the wall. "Dude, we might be in more trouble than we thought. It looks like you broke the wall."

"That was the whole point, *Genius*," Nelson sneered as he walked over to examine Eli's progress.

"Not that wall." Hayden dropped his lumber and made his way across the messy worksite. "This one." He put his hand out and pushed against what appeared to be a depression in the stone. "Whoa." Hayden's eyes widened, and he stepped back, nearly tripping when the wall shifted inward showing a hidden opening.

"Dude! Seriously?" Nelson bounded across the room and stuck his head in the small door. "That's awesome!"

"What is it?" Eli asked as he carefully made his way over.

"Dunno," Nelson grinned over his shoulder. "But we should find out."

Hayden scowled. "Are you serious? There's probably rotting bodies or something in there." He folded his arms across his broad chest. "No, thank you."

Nelson rolled his eyes again. "Rotting bodies? No one has lived here for like a hundred years, any bodies would be complete dust by now, Genius."

"Stop calling me that," Hayden growled.

Nelson's eyebrows shot up. "You're the one who claimed you were so smart, just following your lead... Genius."

Hayden leaned in nose to nose with his little brother. "Don't make me get my carving knives."

Nelson gave a fake shiver. "Ooh, now I'm scared. A guy who spends his time in an apron and puffy hat is gonna hurt me."

Hayden reached out and grabbed Nelson, putting him in a headlock before he could react.

With a laugh and holler, Nelson grabbed Hayden's wrist and twisted his way out, using his years of martial arts training to evade further attempts of imprisonment.

"CHILDREN!" Eli shouted, grabbing them both by the shoulders. "Knock if off for a minute, huh?" His face went back to the hidden door. "I think we should figure out what's going on here." He nodded his chin toward the hole. "If there are hidden rooms, they'll affect the structural integrity of the building and we need to know what we're dealing with."

"True enough," Hayden said, rolling his neck and swinging his arms as if he were warming up for a sports contest.

"Maybe you should stay here, Bro. We wouldn't want to have an accident and hurt your whisking arm or anything," Nelson said with a smirk,

Hayden glared and stepped forward, but Eli stopped him with a hand to his chest. "Where are the flashlights?"

Nelson hurried into the other room and was back in a few seconds. "Here we go! One for each of us. Sorry, Hay, I couldn't find your pretty princess one. It must still be packed in your luggage upstairs." He laughed. "Ouch!" He rubbed the back of his head when Eli slapped him.

"Knock it off, Squirt. One of these days I won't stop him from pounding you into the ground."

"Like a guy who went to school to wear a skirt could pound me," Nelson muttered while rubbing his head.

"For the millionth time! It's an apron! Not a skirt!" Hayden shouted.

Eli turned his flashlight on and pushed the door open as far as it would go. The door was thick and after the first couple of inches, didn't move easily. The squeal of the hinges made it clear that the door hadn't been opened in many years.

With a deep breath, Eli stepped into the darkness. "Oh, man." He coughed a couple of times and swiped in front of his face. "Dang, the dust and cobwebs are thick."

"This is going to be epic," Nelson whispered. "How many dead people do you think we'll find?"

Hayden shook his head. "You're such an idiot."

"And you're such a girl!"

"Shut up," Eli growled. "Nelson, go grab that broom." He put his hand on his hip and flashed his light around. "Maybe I can use it to clear the cobwebs so we can actually walk in there."

"Coming right up, Boss." Nelson worked his way through the construction zone and grabbed a beat up broom sitting in the corner.

"Thanks," Eli murmured as he studied the secret passageway. He looked over his shoulder. "Here we go." Setting his jaw, he held the broom in front of him, swinging it slowly from side to side as he worked his way inside. "There's a staircase in here!" Eli called, surprise evident in his tone.

"Where does it go?" Nelson called back.

Hayden scowled. "How the heck is Eli supposed to know?" He shook his head. "Idiot," he mumbled.

"I meant for him to find out... why are you always so grumpy? You catch more flies with honey than vinegar dude. You, of all people, should know the difference between the two."

Hayden scowled and stepped into the space after Eli.

"Careful, these steps are pretty narrow," Eli's voice echoed slightly as it came up the stone walkway.

"Got it," Nelson yelled, leaning over Hayden's shoulder to answer.

Hayden flinched and covered the offended ear. Grumbling something under his breath, he stepped further into the darkness.

Slowly, the three brothers made their way down the dark and musty stairwell. The air felt heavy with moisture, and an aura of tension settled on each brother as they continued down the seemingly never-ending stairwell.

"This place is creepy." Nelson said as he glanced behind him at the darkness. "Oof!" Just as he turned back around he ran into something solid. "Dude! Why did you stop?" Nelson rubbed his chin where he had smacked into Hayden's head.

"Watch where you're going and you won't have that problem," Hayden muttered. "Eli stopped, so I stopped."

"There's a door," Eli called from the front.

All three brothers focused their flashlight beams to the front. A solid wood door, tall and straight, stood before them.

"Is it locked?" Hayden asked, his normally taciturn voice had lightened to awe.

Eli put his hand out and rested it on the dusty knob. Flexing his muscles, he twisted hard and the heavy door opened slightly. A puff of cold air hit the brothers in the face.

"Whoa..." Nelson breathed.

Eli glanced over his shoulder, his eyebrows furrowed together, before taking a deep breath and shouldering his way into the room.

"Eli? You still alive?" Nelson called out after a few moments of silence.

Hayden elbowed his baby brother in the chest. "Can you shut up for once?"

"What?" Nelson rubbed his chest. "It's a legitimate question."

Hayden looked at the ceiling and shook his head. "Come on," he growled. Slowly, they walked into the dark room.

Eli was standing only a few feet inside the doorway, still as a statue.

"What's going on?" Hayden slapped a hand on Eli's shoulder.

Eli's jaw was slack and his eyes focused into the darkness. Without saying a word, he pointed a finger in front of him. Nelson and Hayden followed his finger and focused their flashlights the same direction as their older brother.

Hayden's eyes widened and Nelson gasped.

"Dude, are you all seeing this?" Nelson's voice was quiet and shaky.

Both of his brothers nodded, but didn't speak.

"I don't think we're desperate anymore," Eli finally mumbled.

CHAPTER 1

Hazel Thurgood glared at the computer screen. The small, black line sitting on the blank page seemed to mock her, and she was getting tired of it.

What is wrong with me? Why can't I think of anything? She pushed her computer glasses back up her nose and chewed on the edge of a pencil she kept handy for notes when writing. *Come on, come on!* Her fingers twitched over the keyboard, but still nothing happened.

"Aargh!" she finally yelled. Pushing back from her desk, she stormed out of her home office and headed toward the kitchen where she grabbed a pint of her favorite ice cream and took it to the family room. Grabbing the remote, she turned on her favorite movie and dug into the cold, chocolatey goodness in her hands.

"Maybe, good, ole Wesley will provide some inspiration," she muttered.

Truth was, Hazel had been struggling with writer's block for weeks. A true romantic at heart, her seemingly endless well of fictional love stories seemed to have dried up. She had struggled with a story before just as any writer does, but never for so long. Usually she struggled to get past a certain scene, but right now, she couldn't even get started. Her last book had come out three months ago and she hadn't put another word to paper since. *Word to screen would be more accurate,* she thought glumly.

For the next couple of hours, she allowed herself to overindulge not only in sugar, but in movie magic. She closed her eyes and thought about what it would be like to be as adventurous and strong as the leading lady in the movie was.

After a moment she huffed a laugh. "Come on, Hazel. Your idea of adventure is handling rush hour traffic. You've never even been camping."

Hazel had been born and raised in the city and had never strayed from the lifestyle. She came from a large, middle-class family who lived in Vancouver, Washington, just across the river from where she now owned her own small home in the suburbs of Portland. Although she had never lacked for necessities, they hadn't had a lot of extra either. Trips to the coast where they stayed in cheap hotels, were about as fancy as her family ever got.

According to Hazel's mother, Hazel was the dreamer of the family. As a child her head was always been in the clouds or a book. Her demeanor might be shy and quiet, but her imagination now paid the bills and Hazel was proud of it. She wrote contemporary romances with strong heroines who were unafraid of life and most importantly, unafraid of love. Which they always found with hunky, alpha males, of course.

Hazel sighed and dropped the spoon in the container. "Essentially, they're everything I'm not." She froze for a moment. An idea started to simmer in her head and she slowly sat up from her slouched position. "Maybe that's it. I've run out of material because I'm so different from my characters." She chewed on the inside of her cheek. "But what if..." She scrunched her freckled nose. "What if I did something that was more like them? What if I went on an adventure? Maybe that would trigger a new story."

She began to tap her foot rapidly as she thought through the idea. "That could work. Right? I mean, what would it hurt?" She stared out the window at the grey, rainy skies. "If nothing else, it would at least help make my descriptions more accurate. If I want to write about adventures, then I need to go on adventures." She pursed her lips and nodded her head emphatically. "It's as simple as that. I can't continue to write about what I don't know."

Standing up, she dumped the empty ice cream container in the garbage and headed back to her office.

For two days, Hazel spent most of her waking hours researching different activities. Everything from skydiving to scuba diving. She debated staying close versus flying across seas. She read reviews, she made comparison charts, and kept an eye on her bank account. Even though she could write much of this off as a business expense, being an independent author meant that her paycheck could fluctuate and being careful was part of her cautious nature.

"Gee whiz," Hazel said as she grabbed some carrot sticks out of the fridge. "Who knew looking up a vacation could be so draining?" Tossing one of the vegetables into her mouth, she crunched down while firing up her social media pages. She absentmindedly scrolled through her feed while snacking when an advertisement ran across her screen.

Whoa. What was that? She slowly moved the screen back up. "Avangarde Castle and Resort." Her eyes widened at the picturesque post of a nearly white, stone castle sitting amongst thick greenery. "Avangarde, Avangarde." She pursed her lips. "Where have I heard that before?" She tapped her foot.

Unable to grasp the memory of the name, she tapped on the ad. A stunning array of photos popped up and Hazel found herself nearly drooling as she went through them. Lush gardens and a walking maze sat on the back of the property. *Just right for a romantic, midnight stroll.* A stone fountain with a circular drive created a luxurious ambience in the front. The chandelier in the attached restaurant nearly made her drop the phone. "Oh. My. Gosh. I don't even want to know how long it takes to clean all those crystals."

When she reached the end of the slide show, a picture of three men popped up. "The Truman brothers! Of course!" Hazel slapped her forehead and shook her head. "I can't believe I didn't remember that."

There probably wasn't a single person, more particularly a woman, in the world who hadn't heard the story of the Truman brothers and their miraculous find. "What are the odds of finding a hidden treasure and becoming instant billionaires?" Hazel shook her head. Her eyes trailed over the three brothers. It was easy to see they were family. All three men had dark hair and were fairly tall. One brother had a couple of inches in height and width on the others, but the firm jaw and straight nose could have been exchanged on any of them and no one would have noticed a difference.

Her eye was caught by the brother on the far right and she scanned the caption. "Nelson Truman..." She rolled the name around on her tongue. "Mmm... sounds like one of my book heroes." Nelson was the smallest of the brothers, with a more wiry build and longer hair, but it was easy to see that he filled out his suit very nicely despite not having the same bulk as the others.

All the brothers were extremely handsome, which is part of why the world had gone so crazy when their story hit the media. They had been dubbed the "Overnight Billionaire Bachelors" and the ladies had been swooning ever since. *Although, two of the brothers are off the market, I believe.* "Only Nelson is unattached," she murmured.

Her eyes kept going back to his grin. Of all the brothers, his was the most genuine. His smile was wide, playful and slightly cocky. "He'd make a fantastic leading man," Hazel giggled.

She dug around a bit more on the website and discovered that not only did they boast a Michelin star restaurant, but they offered adventure tours through their private forest lands. Hazel's jaw dropped when she discovered that Nelson ran the activities side of the resort. "What are the odds?" Her foot began tapping as her mind whirled. "I wonder..." Clicking on the schedule, she noticed that one of the options was a five day camping trip, which included hiking, ATV riding and other outdoor activities.

Her eyes lit up and she let out a little squeal. "This is it. I can feel it!" It took her no time at all to find the button for bookings. After reading all the information, she whistled low under her breath. "Geez.

That's a bit more than I wanted to spend." Her foot went back to its frantic rhythm. The longer she stared at the screen, the faster her heartbeat became. Her lips pinched into a white line before she blew out a harsh breath of air. "Just once. The odds of me doing this again are so slim. Just once I need to live without worry. Nothing ventured, nothing gained." Quickly, she typed in her information and pressed the submit button. "There. Now I can't back out of it." She grinned. "Now it's time to pack." She let out another squeal and rushed to her bedroom to start looking through her clothes.

CHAPTER 2

"Do you really think a camping trip that long is wise?" Eli tapped his fingers on the desk as he considered his younger brother.

Nelson rolled his eyes. "It's already a done deal, Bro. I put it up a few weeks ago and already have an entire crew booked for next week."

"You didn't think that was something you should pass by the group before you took the leap?" Eli glared at him.

"Why? You guys run your sections, I run mine!" Nelson frowned. "And I do a darn good job of it. My part of the resort is always busy."

Eli sighed. "You're right, it is and you have. But this affects more than just you. Hayden usually does your food for the overnighters and this is five days worth of food instead of two. With you gone that long, we need someone to run the rest of the activities here at the resort." He ran his fingers through his hair. "Do you see what I mean? This requires a lot of work and preparation."

Nelson shook his head. "When are you guys ever going to take me seriously? I know all that. I've already told Hayden what I'll need. We're not actually packing the entire week's worth of food on us. One of my workers will be coming up midweek with a delivery. And I've left my right-hand man in charge. I've hired a couple of temp workers to handle cleaning the barns this week so my regular guys can run the activities instead." He huffed and folded his arms. "You guys still treat me like I'm a child."

Eli gave him a pointed stare. "While I'm glad to hear you have thought ahead, you act like a child most of the time."

"Enjoying the lighter side of life does not mean I act like a child."

"Other than this one, what's the longest amount of time you've ever held down a job, Nelson?" Eli raised an eyebrow. "Or stuck with anything that was difficult? You've always jumped from adventure to adventure, never setting down any roots or gaining any traction in life. Don't you think you're old enough to settle down?"

"First of all, not staying in jobs I didn't enjoy doesn't mean I *can't*, it just means I knew when to look for something better. I mean, seriously, I'm here aren't I? I helped build this resort from the ground up and I'm still running my portion of it. And by settling down, what do you mean? Are you talking marriage?" Nelson laughed. "Just because you and Hay got yourselves leg-shackled doesn't mean I have to follow suit. I don't think that's going to be the life for me for a long time yet."

Eli smirked and leaned back in his leather office chair. "One of these days I'm going to be able to rub that comment in your face."

"You wish," Nelson retorted with a laugh.

Eli tapped his desk with a pencil. "Well, it appears you have everything in hand. So, I guess I don't have anything to complain about. But next time I would like a little more warning, please."

Nelson walked to the door and reached for the knob. "Yeah, well, I've learned with you it's better to ask forgiveness than permission." He laughed and ducked out the door quickly when Eli threw his stress ball at him. Nelson kept laughing as he heard it thud against the door behind him.

As he sauntered through the castle, heading to the backdoors, his mind rehashed their conversation. "There's nothing wrong with not being a grumpy old dude," Nelson muttered. "Some men just aren't meant to be stuck in one place or with one person."

Nelson grinned at a couple of the hotel maids as he passed, leaving them giggling into their hands. He smirked and added a bit more strut to his walk. *See? There's nothing wrong with enjoying the attention of everyone, instead of focusing on just one.*

Once outside, Nelson headed for the barns. "Tom, my main man! What's up?"

A middle aged man with an aged cowboy hat on approached and shook Nelson's hand. "Not much, Mr. Truman."

"Nelson."

Tom nodded. "Mr. Truman."

Nelson rolled his eyes good naturedly. Tom was a stickler for propriety and he refused to call his boss anything other than mister.

"We're having the ATVs you need for next week serviced and cleaned up. Next we need to start sorting and packing backpacks and gear. All the sleeping bags are back from the laundry, so it's just a matter of separating it all out."

"Perfect. Geez, you're going to put me out of a job if you keep this up."

Tom gave a crooked grin. "Nah. The girls need a pretty face to look at and my old mug isn't going to do the job. Not to mention the fact that the missus would tan my hide if I modeled myself out."

Nelson burst out laughing. He leaned down and rested his hands on his knees as he enjoyed Tom's comment. Nelson stood straight and wiped at his eyes. "Tom. Never change, Man. Never change."

Tom smiled and shook his head. "You heading up the ride this afternoon? Or one of the young, hired bucks?"

"I'm on it. I just need to get to my office and look through my notes. It's only a two-hour tour, so it's no big deal. However, tomorrow someone else is going to have to do it. I want in on the four-wheeler ride."

Tom nodded. "Sounds good."

Nelson headed to his air-conditioned office at the back of the barn. With a sigh he settled into his comfortable leather chair. They had built the office sparing no expense. His walls were thick enough to hide the noise of the barn and his air system was only for his space, keeping the smell of the animals where it belonged.

Shiny hardwood floors, gleamed in the sunlight shining through the large picture window on the far side of the office, across from the desk. Nelson squinted at the bright light, but let his eyes wander to the outer view. The barn was on the edge of the cleared property, which gave Nelson an open view of mountain and forest.

He leaned back in his chair and put his hands behind his head. "This is the life. Different activities every day and views of a God-created landscape." He sighed. "Let my brothers get married and produce the kidlets. I've already found where I belong."

CHAPTER 3

Hazel's dark blue eyes were wide as she looked around her hotel room. *It's just as gorgeous as the rest of the castle.* Her eyes trailed over the large bed with a grey bedspread that looked thick enough to be a pillow. She whistled low under her breath. "I should go on adventures more often." She grinned. "But first I gotta get more books out if I'm going to afford that."

She dropped her suitcase on the ground and started to walk around. Her fingers trailed over the silver filigree on the lamps that matched the motifs on the fabric of the two large, wingback chairs nestled in the corner.

An ornate writing desk stood in all its antique glory with a quill and ink jar decorating one corner on a silver tray. Hazel gasped and hurried over to inspect the objects, noticing the same design from before on the outer edge of the tray. "Oh my word. This is nuts! Did they have everything custom made?" She blew a raspberry through her lips. "Duh. They're billionaires, of course they did."

She shook her head and ran a hand through her long, windblown hair. Wispy pieces of blonde were sticking to the side of her face and starting to irritate her. Grabbing a hair band out of the back pocket of her jeans, she threw it up in a messy bun on top of her head. "Whew. Nothing like getting all that weight off your neck."

She ventured into the bathroom and nearly swooned in delight. A clawfoot tub sat in the corner, next to a glass shower stall lined with white marble. The shower matched the marble on the counter where a crystal vase filled with white lilies perched. Thick, white, fluffy towels were rolled and stacked on a rack on the wall. Bottles of lotion and shampoo were displayed prettily on another silver tray.

"Too bad I only get to stay here one night," Hazel murmured. "This place is magical!" The package she had purchased included a one-night stay before and after the camping trip so guests didn't have to travel early in the morning to arrive at the resort or leave as soon as they got back.

Rushing to her purse, she pulled out a notebook and pen and started making notes about the room and luxury she had seen coming in. *You never know when you need these kinds of details for a story.*

For the next hour she described the castle and all her feelings on the small piece of paper. Flexing her cramping hand, she set her things down and wandered to the large window. "Oh my word, it does exist!" She sucked in a breath as she discovered her window overlooked the garden maze. "Mmm... walking through one of those aisles with a handsome man? Heavenly. I'll have to use that in a book as well." She narrowed her eyes and glanced at her cell phone for the time. "Maybe there's still time to walk through it today?"

Her stomach grumbled, and she moaned. "Or not. By the time I get dinner, it'll probably be dark and it would be just my luck to get completely lost where no one would find me until morning."

With one last longing glance at the maze, she grabbed her room key and headed downstairs to try out the fancy restaurant. "Maybe I'll even see one of the Truman brothers," she whispered to herself before grinning. *Not like I'd have the courage to speak to one, but who doesn't love seeing a handsome man in person?*

Hazel took her time walking through the halls of the castle on her way to the restaurant. It was obvious whoever designed the castle had taken great pains to make every detail exquisite.

The same filigree that had adorned her room could be found in touches throughout the entire hotel. Large paintings with ornate, antique looking frames perched on the walls. There were very few faces in the frames, mostly landscapes and seascapes.

Hazel admired one particularly detailed painting of a sailing ship on the ocean. She could almost feel the ocean breeze blowing through her hair and smell the salt on the air. Filled with a peace she hadn't felt for awhile, Hazel turned to go to continue on her way.

"Oof!" She bounced off a body and stumbled back a few steps. "I'm so sorry!" Hazel automatically blurted out as she righted herself. Her eyes shot to whoever had been in her path and she began to blink rapidly. *Oh. My. Lanta. It's him. He's even better than his picture.*

Nelson Truman stood in front of her with a crooked grin on his suntanned face. "Sorry. I wasn't paying attention to where I was going," he said in a smooth baritone voice.

Say something! Hazel tried to speak but her tongue seemed glued to the roof of her mouth and there wasn't enough moisture available to unstick it. "Mmmm... yeah..." She trailed off lamely. *You've got to be kidding me.* She mentally facepalmed herself. *That's it? That's all you can say?*

Nelson's grin faded a touch, and he eyed her with a confused grin. "Okay, then." He nodded. "I'll be sure to be more careful in the future. Well, then..." His gorgeous brown eyes darted around. "If you're alright?" He raised an eyebrow.

Hazel nodded jerkily, her mouth still refusing to cooperate.

"I guess I'll just be on my way then." He ran a hand through his thick, dark hair and Hazel sighed out loud at the display of muscles in his arms.

She gasped and threw her hand over her mouth. *Oh sure. Now you decide to work. Stupid mouth.* She could feel a blush creeping over her fair skinned cheeks.

Nelson's eyes widened, and he laughed. "Alrighty then. Take care." Still chuckling, Nelson stepped around her and continued down the hall in the opposite direction of the restaurant.

Hazel couldn't stop herself from turning to watch him walk away. *He is just like the heroes in my books. Good gravy. I could write odes for days about a man like that.*

At the end of the hall, Nelson turned left and glanced back at her, catching her staring at him. A smirk crossed his face as he disappeared from view.

When he was gone, Hazel gave into the earlier impulse and smacked her palm on her forehead. "Great. Now he thinks you're just a star struck idiot." She paused. "Although, to be fair. I guess I was. So I can't really blame him. Good thing he won't be on the camping trip this week. I'd probably trip and break something any time he walked by."

With a groan of disgust at her idiotic behavior, she turned and continued down the corridor to the restaurant entrance.

Can eyes actually pop out of your head? Because I think mine are in danger of doing just that. Hazel barely blinked as she walked into the gorgeous establishment. She couldn't seem to process all the history and wealth quick enough.

She approached the hostess stand and held up a single finger.

The young lady smiled and grabbed a menu. "If you'll just follow me, Miss?" The hostess waited for her with a patient expression on her face.

"Yeah. Sorry." Hazel clamped her jaw shut and stepped after the pretty, young woman in front of her.

"Don't worry. Happens all the time," the girl said with a grin.

I'll bet it does. Hazel smiled in return. Once seated, she immediately turned to the menu. "Sheesh. I can't even pronounce half of these things."

"Good evening. My name is Evan and I'll be your waiter this evening." A man who looked to be just a few years younger than Hazel's twenty-five years, appeared next to her table with a glass of water. After setting it in front of her, he cocked his head and smiled. "Have you had a chance to look at the menu yet? Do you have any questions or would you prefer more time to peruse?"

"I think I need a bit more time," Hazel said softly. "This is a bit overwhelming."

Evan nodded. "First time here?"

She nodded.

"Would you like some suggestions? Or would you prefer to just figure things out on your own?"

Hazel thought for a moment. "Um… a suggestion or two might be nice." She felt her cheeks heat and groaned inwardly at her telltale blush.

Writing had been the perfect career for Hazel. Not only did she love books and happy ever afters, but in public, she was shy and introverted. She was often a homebody and tended to be slightly awkward in public. *As showcased by my reaction to seeing Nelson Truman only moments ago.* But she had come on this trip to step out of her comfort zone and she was determined to make the most of it.

"Great. Well, if you enjoy seafood, the shrimp linguine is my absolute favorite. Always cooked to perfection. If you enjoy red meat, then I recommend the filet. You also can't go wrong with-"

"The pasta sounds great. I'll have that," Hazel interrupted. *Giving me too many choices would have been just as bad as leaving me with the menu.*

Evan smiled and nodded. "One shrimp linguine coming right up. Can I get you something else to drink?"

"Water is great. Thanks."

With a nod, her waiter headed across the dining hall.

Hazel fought the urge to pull out her phone and tuck herself away in a book world while she waited. Instead, she forced herself to look around. The tapestries on the walls were magnificent and the chandelier stunning. Her eyes flitted around to the other inhabitants of the restaurant and she noticed with a sigh of relief that many of them seemed to just be commonplace people like her. Occasionally she saw a couple who were dressed to match the elegance of the castle, but there were far more pairs of jeans than dresses present.

It's probably other guests at the resort, just like me. As her eyes wandered, they suddenly got caught by another pair looking straight at her. A man who appeared to be in his late twenties was watching her and when their eyes met, he smirked. He sat at a table by himself, dressed in a buttondown shirt and jeans. His hair was styled just right and at first glance it was easy to see he was fairly handsome, but the smirk he sent her way reeked of arrogance and set Hazel's teeth on edge.

Crud. Hazel immediately put her gaze back on her table. "That's what I get for trying to get out of my own head." Embarrassment at having been caught people-watching brought heat to her neck and face. In an effort to counteract it, she grabbed her purse and searched for something to write on.

While waiting for her dinner, she began to write notes and ideas for books. Her writing was stiff and jerky and she struggled to concentrate. *I can feel him watching me.* Trying to be subtle, she glanced sideways toward the man.

Sure enough, he was still watching her and grinning.

Hazel snapped her eyes back to her paper. *Shoot. Hopefully he doesn't take eye contact as an invitation.*

Suddenly her mind flooded with thoughts and news stories of women who had traveled alone and never come home. As the first stirrings of panic began to flutter in her chest, Evan arrived with her food.

"Here we are. One plate of shrimp linguini for the lady." He set the plate down and backed up. "Anything else I can get you?"

Evan's polite words and friendly personality helped calm Hazel's worry. *I'm in the middle of a busy restaurant. Nothing is going to happen to me.* "This looks great. Thanks."

Evan nodded and spun on his heel, returning the way he had come.

Leaning down, Hazel took a deep smell of the dish in front of her. "Oh man. That's amazing." Closing her eyes, she said a brief prayer and then dug in. She had to forcibly keep herself from moaning out loud at the deliciousness of the food. "Whoever created this dish needs to get a 'go directly to heaven' card," she muttered around a mouthful.

"Maybe it's you who's from heaven," a deep voice stated.

Hazel jerked her gaze up and almost lost the food in her mouth at the sight of the man who had been watching her.

Still smiling, he slid in the seat across from her.

Hazel choked as she forced the mouthful of food down her throat. Coughing lightly, she grabbed for her water glass and took a big gulp. "Excuse me?" she asked when she could talk.

The man shrugged. "I heard you talking about heaven, so I thought I'd give my own two cents." His eyes danced and that never-ending smirk continued to play on his lips.

Hazel frowned. *Sheesh, conceited much? Who just sits down at someone else's table without asking permission?* "I'm sorry. Do I know you?"

The man held his hand out across the table. "Jack. Jack Weathersby."

Hazel still felt unsettled, but she tentatively put her hand in his. "Hazel." *No way I'm giving him my last name.*

"Hazel. That's a pretty name." He glanced around before bringing his eyes back to hers. "You here all alone?"

Red flags waved through Hazel's vision. *I can't just say nothing. What do I do?* She cleared her throat. "My, uh, my boyfriend isn't with me tonight." She cringed internally. *I hate lying.*

Jack plastered that smirk back on his face and sat back in his seat. "I see. Well, I'm by myself too. I'm sure you don't mind if I join you? Cute girls shouldn't sit alone. This way we're not quite so lonely, right?"

He's not getting the hint and I don't like guys who are aggressive. But how do I get rid of him?

"Miss?" Evan's voice broke through her thoughts. "Is everything all right here?"

Relief flooded Hazel at Evan's obvious concern.

"Things are great. Can we get a dessert menu?" Jack piped up.

Hazel felt the blood drain from her face and she began to panic at the guy's dominating attitude.

Evan's eyes darted to Jack and then back to Hazel's. His eyebrows were furrowed, and he pinched his lips. "I think maybe the lady would like to dine alone," he said.

Jack raised an eyebrow. "Look, no one asked your opinion. Your job is to bring us the food. Got it?"

Hazel could see the anger rising in both men and she felt nauseous. *Guess that's one way to get rid of an appetite.* "Actually, I need to go," she blurted out.

Both men jerked their heads toward her.

"I, uh, I can't eat another bite." She slipped out of her seat and slapped a bill on the table. "Good night."

Doing her best to hurry without actually running, Hazel made her way back to her room. Once there, she leaned against the door and took some deep, relaxing breathing. "And this is why I stay home. There are total weirdos out here." She stood and grabbed her pajamas out of her suitcase. "Good thing I'm heading out with the camping trip tomorrow. I won't have to see that guy ever again."

NELSON CHUCKLED TO himself yet again as he thought of the girl he encountered in the hallway. At first he had been concerned that something was wrong, but when the blush crept up her cheeks and she stumbled over her words, he could see it was nothing more than being in awe.

He had seen the reaction many times over the past couple of years, after he and his brothers had been dubbed the "Overnight Billionaire Bachelors", but never had he found the scene quite so cute as he had this afternoon.

He thought back on the girl's wide blue eyes and her bright blonde hair, which looked natural. She'd had it pulled up in one of those buns girls wear. Her lips were full and pale pink. Her fair skin had turned a deep shade of red, even covering the burst of freckles across her nose.

All in all, she was exactly what Nelson's mom would have called 'cute as a button'. "If she'd had enough courage to speak, it would have been fun to flirt with her a bit," he mused. As it was, he was worried she would faint if he'd said anything else.

Nelson turned off his car as he parked in Eli's driveway. His sister-in-law, Ivy, had invited him and the rest of the family over for dinner. Everyone was coming in order to discuss moving their sisters from their college apartments to the resort.

In true Nelson fashion, he burst into the home, rather than knocking. "I know you missed me, Fairy Girl!"

Ivy's answering laugh could be heard from the kitchen area, while Eli's groan sounded in the background.

Nelson grinned and shut the door behind him before moving further into the house. "Mmm... smells good in here," he said as he sniffed the air.

"Hey, Nellie. Long time, no see," Ivy said with a grin as she took a casserole dish out of the oven.

He and Eli exchanged chin raises. Plopping himself in a stool at the bar, Nelson rested his arms on the counter top. "So, where's everyone else?"

"Hayden and Cadence will be here soon. Hayden had to check on the restaurant, first."

Nelson leaned back. "I'm actually pretty surprised we got him to come to dinner. He never leaves his baby."

Ivy shrugged. "It wasn't that hard. Ever since he and Cadence got married, he's worked harder to keep a steady schedule so he's home more. No more twenty-four-hour kitchen marathons."

"Ah. True love." Nelson held a hand to his chest. "Just what every man needs to tie him down."

"Watch it," Eli muttered with a pointed glare.

Nelson put up his hands and his best innocent face. "What?"

Eli put his eyes heavenward and muttered under his breath.

Haha. He's so easy to annoy. It's like taking candy from a baby. Nelson grinned.

"We're here!" Cadence's voice called from the front room.

"Oh, good! Dinner is just now ready." Ivy picked up a dish and started taking it to the table. "Come on in and sit down!" she hollered.

"It smells delightful," Cadence said as she walked in, slipping out of her coat.

Hayden grabbed the coat with his free hand and helped his wife finish removing it, before setting a pan on the counter. "Lasagna?" he asked Ivy as he sat at the table.

"Yep." Ivy chewed her lip. "I know it can't compare to yours, but hopefully you won't hate me when we're done."

Hayden chuckled. "If yours was as good as mine, I'd have wasted all those years at culinary school. Oof!" He grinned when his wife elbowed him in the ribs. "I'm sure it's delicious."

"Much better. Good boy," Cadence said, patting Hayden on the head.

The table cracked up with laughter while Hayden glared playfully at his wife.

After grace was said and everyone had dished up, they picked up the topic they were meeting for.

"So," Eli began "the girls are done, and I think we need to just move them up here and take care of them. Mom and Dad would have loved to see us all together."

There was a moment of silence at the mention of their parents who had been killed in a car accident right after the twins, Laken and Teagan, had left for college. They had gone on their first trip as empty nesters and were hit when a drunk driver ran a red light, killing them instantly.

Nelson nodded while he chewed.

Cadence cleared her throat. "You just want them to come and live? They aren't going to want jobs?"

Ivy narrowed her gaze at Eli. "I know you want to take care of them, but they're adult women and they both just finished their educations. They aren't going to want to be taken care of. You once mentioned to me the thought of building a spa and a greenhouse. Is that not still on the table?"

"A greenhouse would be perfect with the restaurant," Hayden said. "I know we discussed it awhile ago, but it's never really come up again. Teagan could grow me produce year round, but still have time for the fancy, experimental stuff she does."

Ivy pointed her fork at him. "Exactly. She would have a purpose. She's going to want that. They both are. I, personally, also think a spa would be a fantastic addition to the resort."

Eli looked at Cadence. "Could you put together some numbers and see if those ideas are feasible? I know, technically, we can do it, but it will take awhile for the profits to come back and I don't want to put ourselves in a bad position."

Cadence nodded. "I can run some projections of what a P&L statement might look like over the next twelve, thirty-six, and sixty months to give us a better idea of feasability, but I really don't think it will be a problem. The resort has been doing well and our balance sheets have done nothing but move forward."

Nelson leaned back and blinked at Cadence. "I didn't know you spoke another language."

Cadence rolled her eyes and smiled. "Whatever," she muttered good naturedly.

"Careful, your inner geek is showing. It doesn't quite match the rest of you."

Ivy laughed, but Hayden gave Nelson a glare.

Nelson grinned widely then asked, "Who would we use as a builder?"

Hayden wiped the red sauce from his lips. "We could use Jaxson again."

"He still working?" Eli grinned. "I thought he might have retired after the paycheck he got for doing the castle."

Hayden frowned. "You'd think, huh? But he ended up spending most of it in a custody battle over his son."

Ivy set down her fork. "How sad. Did he win?"

Hayden nodded. "Yeah. But he'll be hurting for a long while yet. I'm sure he's looking for any job he can get."

Eli tapped the glass in his hands. "I don't have any problems with that. He did good work before and I have no reason to think we won't get the same result this time." He looked around the table. "That sound all right with everyone?"

Nods and murmurs of agreement sounded around the table.

"Great. I'll call and talk to the girls tomorrow and we'll discuss getting them here. I'm sure they'll both want to have some input about the design of their work spaces."

Nelson snickered. "You might not want to tell Laken that Jaxson is coming. She'll probably decide to tour the world or something."

Hayden rolled his eyes. "She can get over it. He's been my best friend since we were kids and I'm not about to push him aside because of Miss Priss."

Ivy paused with a piece of garlic bread right in front of her mouth. "What's the problem?"

"Oh, nothing," Nelson said with a grin. "Just that Laken can't stand Jaxson. Every time they're in the same room sparks fly and not the good kind."

"He thinks she's a spoiled brat, and she thinks he's a jerk," Eli explained. "But it will be fine. We'll just keep them apart as much as possible."

"Good luck with that," Nelson muttered.

"Whatever," Hayden growled. "She'll just have to grow up."

"Where's the fun in that?" Nelson laughed.

"Kind of like that guy in the restaurant tonight," Cadence grumbled.

"What do you mean? What happened in the restaurant?" Eli asked.

"Some idiot tried to get too friendly with a girl who was there by herself." Hayden shook his head. "Evan, one of my waiters, tried to help, but apparently she bolted even though she had only just started her meal."

Nelson frowned. "That's not right."

"What's worse is that she threw some cash down on her way out." Cadence pinched her lips. "She shouldn't have had to pay tonight but without a check or credit card we don't know her name in order to credit the money back to her."

"Men like that drive me crazy." Ivy grimaced. "Sometimes we're just not interested." She stabbed at her salad.

"And sometimes we are interested but the men are too dumb to notice," Cadence added with a wink.

Nelson coughed to cover his laugh as both Hayden and Eli glared at their wives.

"Dessert anyone?" Ivy said with a wide, innocent grin.

Hayden jerked his head around. "Wait a minute, I thought I was bringing dessert."

"You were. I was just trying to change the subject." She put a bite of pasta in her mouth.

"Chocolate, a classic deflection," Cadence agreed.

"You guys better be careful. These ladies are running circles around you," Nelson said with a smirk.

"Or so we let them think," Hayden said as he leaned back in his seat. He laughed when Cadence smacked him in the shoulder. Leaning over, he gave her a quick kiss on the cheek. "I'll grab the pie."

"I'll grab the plates," Cadence offered.

Together they walked into the kitchen and appeared a few minutes later with their supplies.

"Ooh, that looks delicious," Ivy gushed.

"Oh, it is," Cadence smiled. "I had nothing to do with it."

Nelson snorted at his sister-in-law's joke. Cadence may be able to punch numbers with the best of them, but she was quickly discovering that she had zero skills in the kitchen. *Good thing she married Hayden, Le Chef Extraordinaire.*

"What time do you leave in the morning?" Eli asked as he accepted a plate of pie.

Nelson jerked his head up. "Me?"

Eli nodded.

"We've told the campers to gather at nine, we'll take off a half hour later, hopefully."

"Your food packs are ready," Hayden said. "Just send someone to the kitchens when you're ready."

"Thanks," Nelson said around a mouthful.

"Did you bring extra sunscreen and stuff for people who forget theirs?" Ivy asked.

Nelson sighed and nodded. "Yes, Mom. We've got everything we need."

"Well excuse me, Nellie." Ivy teased with a grin. "I just think about how often people call the front desk about things they forgot. Some of it is ridiculous."

"I'll bet," Cadence murmured.

"We sent out a list of supplies to everyone going, so hopefully most of them followed it pretty closely. But we do have extras of the essentials and we're not that far from the resort if we have an emergency."

"Where exactly are you setting up camp?" Hayden inquired.

"In that valley by the pond. The waterfall isn't far from there, there are plenty of trees for privacy, and I'll take them swimming and rappelling while we're there as well."

"Sounds like a fun time," Ivy grinned.

"That's the plan," Nelson grinned as he polished off his pie. "That's the plan."

CHAPTER 4

Hazel's knees were shaking as she hefted her backpack on. Last night she had transferred the necessary items into the pack and this morning she had taken her suitcase out to her car.

Pushing her sunglasses onto her nose, she began to walk around the castle to the barn where those going on the camping trip were meeting. *Okay. I'm a big girl. I can do this. People step outside their comfort zones all the time and very rarely do they die.*

She nearly turned her feet back around at the errant thought. *Oh my word. I'm going to be out in the wilderness where there are wild animals! What if something tries to eat me? Or what if a mosquito bites me and gives me malaria? What was I thinking? I'm a sit-at-home-and-read type of girl! I don't have adventures!*

Gritting her teeth, Hazel forced her feet to keep moving forward. "Come on, Hazel. You already paid for this. It would be so stupid to back out now. For once in your life, be brave!"

Several other people were already gathered in front of the barn and Hazel headed in their direction. As she got closer, a man came out of the structure and walked over to her. "That your pack?"

"Uh... yep."

"Great. You can just set it with the other equipment, right there." He pointed toward other duffles and backpacks.

"Th-thanks," Hazel stuttered.

By the time she came back to the group, the man was off helping someone else. *I wonder if he's the one running this? Too bad the handsome Nelson Truman won't be here.* Hazel held back the grin that wanted to cross her lips. *I could certainly handle a week in his presence.* She thought of their meeting last night. *Or not. I'd probably just make a worse impression than I did last night.* She closed her eyes and held in a groan. *No. It's best he's not here. That way I won't trip over my feet just looking at his cute face.*

Her eyes wandered around the group. It appeared that some of the people were there together. A young couple were holding hands and Hazel nearly sighed at the sight. *I wonder if they're on their honeymoon?* A man and woman stood to the side with two kids, who looked to be between the ages of twelve and fourteen. The older boy was typing away on his phone and his dad kept shooting him dirty looks. *Ni-iice. Nothing like a techy teenager going through withdrawals while we're away.*

Hazel's eyes continued to skim, noticing several other people appeared to be by themselves, when her gaze jerked to a halt. *No. Please no.* On the far side of the group, talking to another gentleman, was Jack.

"Maybe he's just seeing someone off? I mean, seriously, what are the odds that he would be coming on this too?" Hazel muttered.

Backing up a couple of steps, she tried to stay hidden from his view while still keeping an eye on him. She kept her head ducked down, but used her peripheral vision to watch his movements. When one of the workers came up to take his duffel bag, Hazel's heart sank. *Crud. Now what am I going to do? Can I fend him off all week? Or maybe he got the message last night and he'll be angry with me all week instead. Or maybe miracle of miracles, he'll just ignore me.*

Her attention was caught as a man strutted out of the barn and the murmuring among the crowd picked up. Squinting, Hazel thought the man's walk looked familiar. It was difficult to see his face as he had a baseball hat and sunglasses on, but there was something about him...

"Hello, everyone!" The man's voice boomed across the small area where they stood. "I'm Nelson Truman-"

Hazel gasped and jerked back. *What is he doing here? Doesn't he have people who do this for him?* She took a deep breath. *Okay, Haze, calm down. He's probably just seeing us off. Good hospitality and all that.*

"I'm excited to be heading up our little expedition this week and look forward to getting to know you all."

Well, there went that idea. Hazel felt her world closing in on her. Not only did she have to deal with 'guy who can't take a hint', but now Nelson 'I saw Hazel acting like an imbecile' Truman was going to be with her all week as well. *This has turned into a nightmare.*

She pinched the bridge of her nose. *Maybe I should just get a cat? That's an adventure in and of itself, right?*

She suddenly realized that the group was fairly quiet. Looking around, she noticed all the other heads were searching the group as well.

"Hazel Thurgood? Are you here?" Nelson frowned as he looked down at his clipboard and back up at the crowd.

You've got to be kidding me. "Uh," she cleared her throat, "yeah. Yeah!" She got louder. "I'm here."

Nelson looked over at the sound of her voice and his eyebrows shot up as he recognized her. A slow grin pushed his lips wide and Hazel watched them, mesmerized by their movement. *Who knew a man's lips could be so attractive?*

"Nice to see you again, Hazel," Nelson said before moving on to the next person on the list.

Hazel opened her mouth but was too late. Nelson was already calling out other names. Putting her gaze back down on the ground, she glanced sideways to see if Jack had caught who she was.

It was hard to tell with his sunglasses on, but his gaze appeared to be directed toward her and that same cocky grin from last night was on his face. *Shoot, shoot, shoot. I don't think he's going to ignore me.*

Hazel fidgeted in her spot as Nelson finished the roll call.

Once they were done, Nelson began going over the rules and itinerary. Hazel barely caught any of his words as she was dividing her attention between Nelson and Jack. With the way Jack was watching her, she was afraid he was going to come speak to her as soon as the group was let loose and she couldn't figure out a way to avoid it.

Nelson finally finished talking and announced that they were going to be getting on the four-wheelers. "We have a few more people than ATV's, so some of you will be doubled up. We tried to make sure we kept groups together, though, so no one should have to sit with someone they don't know."

Hazel let out a sigh of relief at the words. *It would be just my luck to have to sit behind Jack.*

Nelson and the other workers began walking around, directing people to the vehicle they would be driving. Hazel watched, waiting for her turn and let her guard down.

"Well, well, well, fancy meeting you here," Jack whispered in her ear.

Hazel jumped back. "Oh! J-Jack! I didn't see you there."

Jack crossed his arms and smirked at her. "I didn't know you would be coming on this trip."

Hazel gave an uneasy laugh and her eyes darted around. "I didn't know you would be either."

"Guess that just means we'll have a chance to get to know each other better." He raised an eyebrow.

"Um... maybe," Hazel tried to smile, but it felt more like a grimace.

She glanced toward the rides and noticed Nelson frowning at her. A blush crept up her cheeks, and she stepped back a little from Jack. *I don't want Nelson to think I'm with him. Wait. What? Why would that matter? It's not like Nelson is going to talk to me or anything. I'm just one of his guests here.*

"Hazel!"

She jerked toward the sound.

Nelson was smiling kindly and Hazel felt her heart flutter a little. *Down girl! He's just like one of your book boyfriends. Rich, handsome and wonderful, but not real.*

Nelson waved her over. "Right over here." He patted the seat.

Hazel couldn't help but smile in return and started to take a step toward him.

"Do you know him?" Jack was frowning at Nelson.

"Uh... yeah..." *I met him last night. That counts, right?*

Jack grunted, but the scowl never left his face.

Hazel darted away from him and walked over to Nelson.

"Hey," he said softly. "Are you okay? You looked pretty uncomfortable."

"Oh, yeah. I'm fine." Hazel felt her blush again. "He was just saying hi."

"Is that your boyfriend?"

"Oh, no!" Hazel's voice was loud and she immediately, ducked her head. "Sorry. No. I, uh, met him last night in the Avangarde restaurant. Here. At the restaurant." *Oh my word, stop talking, stop talking, stop talking!*

Nelson's eyes narrowed, and he glanced between the scowling Jack and her again. "I see," he murmured before changing the subject. "So, do you know how to drive one of these?"

Hazel looked over the four-wheeler. It looked kind of like a wide motorcycle to her with more wheels, but since she had never ridden either, she had no real frame of reference. "I can't say that I do." She scrunched her face. "I didn't see anything about having to have experience on the form. Is that going to be okay?"

"Yeah, yeah. It's fine. I just needed to know how much help to give you."

"Well, considering I've never been camping either, I'll need all the help I can get," Hazel blurted before she could think better of it. *Nice, Haze. Exactly what every instructor wants to hear.*

To her surprise, Nelson smiled wide. "Really? Well, you're in for an adventure then." He frowned quickly. "Are you okay driving one by yourself?"

Hazel pinched her lips. Her introvert voice was screaming that she was crazy and should get out while she can, while the tiny voice that had brought her here in the first place kept telling her to go for it. "Umm..."

"Hey," Jack sauntered up to them. "I couldn't help but overhear that you've never driven one of these before." He glanced quickly at Nelson, who was still frowning, and then back at Hazel with that same cocky grin he'd had on his face since she first met him. "You can always ride with me." He leaned in close and dropped his voice. "I'll teach you everything you need to know."

Hazel's eyes widened, and she squeaked as she stumbled back a few steps. *Oh my gosh. What do I do?*

"Look, buddy," Nelson stepped up to Hazel's shoulder. "You need to back off. The lady is just fine. She doesn't need your help."

"Oh?" Jack folded his arms and glared at Nelson. "And I suppose she needs yours, huh? Think your money makes you better than me?"

"Whoa, whoa, whoa." Hazel's tongue finally unstuck itself from the roof of her mouth. "Look, this is getting out of hand. I will be riding by myself, thank you. I'm sure the instructors can teach me everything I need to know."

Nelson smiled, like he'd won a victory and nodded at Hazel, while Jack continued to give Nelson the stink eye.

"Whatever." He dropped his arms and stepped back. "I'll catch up with you later. When it's not so crowded." Spinning on his heels, he stalked toward his own ATV, sitting down and revving the engine.

Hazel let out a long breath. "Sorry about that. This is why I almost never leave my house."

Nelson burst out laughing and Hazel felt her cheeks flush. *Good grief. What is wrong with me? I'm a writer for heaven's sake. You'd think I could come up with something more suave than blurting out all my dumbest thoughts.*

Nelson took a deep breath as he finally got himself under control. "Okay, well, let's get you settled here. And," he glanced over his shoulder at Jack, "if you feel uncomfortable at all, you have my full permission to come seek me out. I don't like guys who push themselves on women. So you can use me as a shield if necessary. 'Kay?"

Still feeling flushed, Hazel nodded. "Got it. Thank you."

"Right. Now. Why don't you have a seat and I'll give you the basics."

Hazel straddled the four-wheeler and fiddled with her thumbs as Nelson gave her a run down of how to go and stop. At his encouragement, she put her hands on the handlebars and twisted her hand to rev up the engine. "Whoa…" she murmured as the vehicle responded.

"Don't do it too hard once you get going or you'll jump forward. I've seen people shoot their ATV's straight up in the air when they weren't careful," Nelson admonished.

"Slow. Got it." *Oh, man. Why did he have to say that? Now I'm going to be freaked out the whole time that I'm gonna get thrown off a four-wheeler. Not a horse or something with a mind of its own, but a four-wheeler. Something I'm supposed to have complete control over.*

"Hey." Nelson put his hand on her shoulder and smiled. "You got this. It's not hard. You'll do great. And remember to stick close if you need protection, huh?"

Hazel gave one last nod before Nelson turned and went to help the last person get settled.

Here we go. Adventure number one is about to begin.

NELSON WENT THROUGH the usual spiel with the last person he was helping all while his mind was back on the beautiful Hazel Thurgood. Her girl-next-door looks were absolutely adorable, and he found himself attracted to her little sarcastic quips as well.

He had to hold back a laugh as he thought of the things she had said in response to Jack's overbearing personality. The thought of Jack brought back his frown from earlier. *Dude. I hate guys like that. Hazel was clearly uncomfortable and scared and the guy wouldn't take no for an answer. I'll bet he's the same one everyone was talking about from the restaurant last night. Hazel did say that's where they met. I'm going to have to keep an eye on him. She's obviously too nice to put him in his place.*

"Sorry. Am I doing something wrong?" The woman he was helping glanced down at the ATV, then back up at him. "I thought I was following your instructions."

"Oh, sorry. Yeah, you're doing great." Nelson smiled wide. "I was just thinking about something I needed to grab. No worries." He looked around then back. "You all settled then?"

"Sure. Thanks."

Nelson nodded and headed toward his crew. "Got everyone? We've helped those who are doubling up, right?"

"Yeah," Jerome nodded. "Although, that teenage kid on his phone is going to be trouble. He couldn't look up long enough to hear everything."

Nelson frowned, glancing at the boy in question. His dad was standing next to him, speaking in a low voice. *Hopefully, the kid'll listen up long enough for us to get to the campsite.* "Okay, We'll keep an eye on him. Oh." He turned back to his workers. "We also need to watch that Jack guy, plus Hazel."

The four men in front of him eyed each other and grinned.

"Pay up," Daniel said to Jerome, reaching out his hand.

"Aw, Man." Jerome plopped a bill into Daniel's hand. "I always lose."

"Never bet against a pretty woman, Man," Daniel said with a chuckle.

"Guys." Nelson folded his arms. "It's not what you think. Jack is hitting on Hazel and she doesn't like it. Your job is to help me keep him off her back for the week."

"Oh, yeah."

"Got it."

"Uh, huh." Came the multitude of replies.

Nelson rolled his eyes. "Whatever, ya bunch of dorks. Come on. Sun's a-wastin.'"

Nelson hopped onto his own ATV and took off his hat. Waving it in the air, he called for everyone's attention. "Alrighty, folks! Here we go! I'll be in front, Jerome will be in back. There are three other workers who will stay mixed in the middle and are more than happy to help if necessary. Just flag one of us down." With a whoop, he revved his four-wheeler and headed toward the forest trail they were taking.

The loud engines of their transportation drowned out all the natural sounds of the woods, but despite the ringing it caused in his head, Nelson took a deep breath and sighed in contentment. It was the perfect day to start a camping trip. The sun was shining and only a few clouds marred the bright blue sky. *Too bad it won't last. Stupid Pacific Northwest and all its rain.*

He and his crew had had to pack extra shelters and tarps, as the weather forecast showed the sun would only last for the first couple of days. Then it was right back to grey and misty, as per the norm.

Nelson took a quick glance over his shoulder, glancing at the other rider's positions. *I am NOT looking for Hazel,* he reassured himself, even as he scanned for her black baseball cap.

When he didn't easily spot her, he spun back around, keeping his eye on the road. *Dude. She's cute, but your only job is to guide her on the camping trip and protect her from that Jack guy. Nothing else.*

He squinted up at the sun and noticed how the blue sky was almost the exact shade of Hazel's eyes. *Hers are a touch darker. More sapphire. DUDE!* He shook his head. "Knock it off, man. Girls are off limits," he muttered. "Both your brothers are now taken, it's your turn to enjoy the limelight and saddling yourself with a shy, quiet cutie would seriously cut down on your dating life."

He would never admit it, but Nelson had always been intimidated by his brothers. Eli had been responsible since the day he was born and had been his father's pride and joy. The girl's had loved his grey eyes and his chivalrous manners had never left him at a loss for companions. Hayden had always been big and intense and once his football career took off, he became an instant hit among the ladies. "Maybe if I tucked a football helmet under my arm and became dark and brooding, I'd get some attention too," Nelson grumbled.

Even after Hayden had given up football, he had brought himself near celebrity level just from his cooking skills. In fact, Hayden had been kicked out of New York because a woman wasn't willing to take no for an answer.

Nelson knew it was dumb to compare himself to his brothers, but he couldn't help it. While his brothers had made something of themselves, he'd been the wild child. The floater. The one who couldn't hold down a job to save his life. He had flunked out of college because he just couldn't bring himself to care about all those classes, when he'd rather be outside doing something active.

"And according to Eli, you're still playing instead of working." Nelson sighed. "But no more. Now you get to have a little attention. No one cares that you weren't a good student or that you don't have a college degree. Now I'm the only 'Overnight Billionaire Bachelor' left. That means that I'll get the attention and it would be stupid to give that away by getting involved with one girl... even if she is adorable."

The rest of the ride went smoothly. No one ran into anything, no one fell off. During the breaks, everyone paid attention to the instructions and stayed close. Nelson was beginning to think that this camping trip was going to be a breeze.

Once they arrived at the campsite, his crew began to unload and start spreading out the tents.

"Listen up, everyone!" Nelson cupped his hands around his mouth to get the attention of the campers. After they wandered over to where he was standing, he continued. "We have large tents for the families." He waved his arm toward one of his employees. "Daniel is setting those up. So, you guys," he pointed toward the family of four, "will be in that one. You two," he pointed toward one of the couples, "will be over there. And you guys," he pointed toward the last couple, "will be in that tent."

Once they had left, there were only singles standing next to him. "Okay." He rubbed his hands together. "All of our tents are two-man tents. So we are going to pair you up."

Nelson narrowed his eyes as he watched Jack sidle up to Hazel and whisper something in her ear, and Hazel went pale, shaking her head. *He better not be thinking I'll put the two of them in a tent together.* Nelson felt his frustration and protective instincts flare.

"We have an odd number of people, so you two ladies," Nelson pointed toward the young women, "will be paired up. Be ready to become bff's."

The girls smiled wide and giggled at his joke before introducing themselves to each other.

"And Jack, you and Tyler will be rooming together," Nelson finished.

"Wassup man?" Tyler said, slapping Jack on the back.

Jack shot a look at Nelson before tilting his chin up and acknowledging his roommate.

Hazel's worried eyes glanced around. "Umm... Mr. Truman?"

Nelson stepped close. "Just Nelson," he said with a grin.

Hazel's genuine smile brought out the dimple in her cheek and Nelson had the oddest urge to touch it with his finger.

"You didn't assign me a tent," she said softly, snapping Nelson out of his imaginings.

"Yeah," he rubbed the back of his neck, "you're lucky enough to get one to yourself. Since we had an odd number, one person got to win the lottery, and I thought maybe you could use the quiet. You don't seem like the type of person who enjoys all night, girl talk."

That perfect smile crossed her face again. "You're pretty good at reading people. Did you study psychology or something in school?"

Nelson felt a blush creeping into his cheeks, so he cleared his throat and shoved the embarrassment back down. "Nah. It's pretty obvious that you're more on the quiet side."

Hazel sighed and glanced sideways. "I wish others would be as observant."

Nelson narrowed his eyes as Jack and his new buddy laughed over some joke. "What was he saying to you a minute ago?"

Hazel's cheeks turned bright pink and Nelson's suspicion shot up a notch.

"It was nothing. He was just trying to be funny."

Nelson stepped closer so he could whisper. "Look, I'm not trying to pry, but I'd really like you to tell me what he said. I want everyone to have a good time and if I don't know what's going on, I can't fix it."

Her eyes shone in adoration and Nelson felt a surge of pride at her obvious appreciation. "I've never had someone so determined to come to my rescue before. You're just like one of the heroes I wri-" She cleared her throat and stepped back. "Sorry. I didn't need to say that. Um," she chewed her lip. "Jack was just making a joke that he and I could be roomies. But your announcement put an end to that." She spun her head toward him. "Not that I would have taken him up on his offer, anyway. I just meant that with you being in charge and all, your orders made it easier for him to back off."

Nelson felt a muscle in his jaw twitch. *That guy goes too far. She's obviously not interested and he won't stop.* "I'm not okay with someone talking to you like that." When he realized what he'd said, he backtracked. "To *anyone* like that."

Hazel's flushed face grew even darker and Nelson knew he needed to reign it in.

"Alright," he took off his hat and ran his hand through his hair. "Let's put you in the tent closest to mine, that way he won't try anything funny in the middle of the night."

"You think he would do something like that? Really?" Hazel's gorgeous blue eyes were wide and her jaw dropped.

"I have no idea," Nelson said honestly, "but he hasn't been good about taking your rejections, so I don't want to take any chances." He turned and started walking. "Come on. Let's get you settled and if he does anything else outrageous, we'll do something more drastic."

Hazel nodded meekly and started to follow him.

Nelson slowed so she could walk by his side. Her presence was peaceful and calm and he liked the light floral scent wafting off of her. As someone who was always on the go, Nelson very rarely felt like slowing down to smell the flowers, but right now that's all he wanted. *What is wrong with me? This woman is messing with my head!* Shaking his head, he showed her where to put her stuff.

CHAPTER 5

Hazel did her best to set up her gear in the tent. Although the structure had only been up for a few minutes, apparently that was all it took for it to be twenty degrees hotter than outside. The air felt thick and dry and she wondered how she would breathe at night.

It's the first peaceful moment I've had though, so I can't really complain. After setting her backpack off to the side and taking off her sneakers, she stretched herself out on top of the sleeping bag.

"Ahhh... feels good." Her back ached and her neck was sunburned from their ride today. Her hands were also a little sore as she had been gripping the handles like a lifeline for the first hour they drove. Eventually, when she figured out that she wasn't going to crash, she relaxed and was able to enjoy the scenery as they rode.

The mountain trail had been full of trees and wildflowers. "And the wonderful smell of exhaust fumes," she said with a laugh. Being in the middle of the pack had not made it easy to breathe in the fresh, forest air, but it helped her feel safer as they climbed hills.

Exhausted from pushing herself so far out of her comfort zone already, Hazel let her eyes flutter closed. It took no time at all for Nelson's handsome face to appear behind her eyelids.

"Mmm... that man is just delicious. His eyes are always twinkling with mischief and his grin is contagious. He doesn't seem afraid of anything," she murmured with a contented sigh. "The perfect book boyfriend. Especially the way he keeps coming to my aid with Jack." She frowned. *That guy just can't take a hint. I don't want to be rude to him, but I'm not interested. How does he not see that?* "But Nelson... hmm... I'm probably too interested in him."

"Hey, Hazel? You gonna stay in there all day?" Nelson's voice came from the door of her tent and she sat upright with a jerk.

Oh, crud. Please tell me he didn't hear any of that.

"Hazel?" Nelson ventured again.

"Uh, yeah! Coming. Just a sec." She scrambled to get her shoes on and crawled to the front of the tent, unzipping the door. "Ouch," she muttered as her knee hit a rock. She stood and stumbled a bit in her haste, but strong arms grabbed her and kept her from hitting the dirt again.

"Whoa, there. No hurry. I thought for a minute you might be taking a nap, but we're going to walk to the pond and I thought you might want to come." Nelson's deep voice was inviting and sent heat racing through Hazel's body. It was especially concentrated on where his hands were still wrapped around her upper arms.

Oh my goodness. It's just like in the books. A clumsy heroine is saved by a handsome prince. Okay, maybe not prince, but hero. Or whatever. But he's handsome. He's definitely handsome.

Nelson blinked a couple of times. "Did you want to go to the pond, then?"

Hazel shook her head when she realized she was staring like a starstruck idiot... again. "Oh, sorry. Daydreaming." She pushed against every nerve ending in her body when she stepped out of his hands. "Thanks for the save, by the way. What were you asking exactly?"

Nelson was looking at his hands, like they didn't belong to him, before clearing his throat and stuffing them in his jeans. "We, uh, I was going to show everyone where the pond is. Did you want to join us?"

"Oh, that would be lovely. Thank you." She stepped toward her tent door. "Let me just grab my hat." She put her hand to her head and nearly groaned. *I've got nasty hat hair and I've been standing here talking with the most handsome man I have ever met. Lovely. That's definitely not how it would go in the books.*

After stuffing her hair back in the baseball cap she had been wearing, Hazel followed Nelson over to where the rest of the group was waiting.

"I just want to thank everyone for such a good trip up here!" Nelson called out with a smile. "You guys rock! Now, I know we're all hot and sweaty, and the lake isn't far, only a couple minutes walk. Once we're there, please stay close. Believe it or not, there are actually wild animals up here."

Hazel gasped lightly. *Great. Now I have to worry about bears and stuff too. Why did I ever think this would be a good idea?*

"Feel free to get in the lake if you want, or just dip in your toes. But, don't say I didn't warn you! Up here it's all mountain run off and we are pretty close to the snow pack. Doesn't matter how long that sun's been beating down, it's not even close to being warm. It's fun if you're brave enough, but definitely cold. Got it?"

A general murmur sounded throughout the group and one weird cough. Hazel frowned and glanced at the sound, only to realize it was Jack. He had his fist to his mouth, hiding a smile. As if he felt her looking at him, his eyes met hers and he dropped the fist, winking in invitation.

Hazel's ever present blush crept back up her cheeks at being caught staring. Clearing her throat, she turned back to Nelson who was leading everyone to the path they were going to take.

Hazel plodded along behind the family of four and couldn't help but overhear their conversation. She bit her lips to keep from snickering at the complaints of the oldest son. Apparently, there is no wifi signal this high in the mountains and he was not happy about it. *What did he expect? That's probably the whole reason his parents brought him out here, just to get him to look up from his phone.*

"Hey," a feminine voice caught Hazel's attention, and she turned to see who was speaking to her. "I'm Mallory and this is Annette."

Hazel smiled. "Hi, I'm Hazel."

The women both looked to be in their late teens or early twenties. Each of them had a ready smile and bubbly personality. *Exactly the kind of person to be a heroine in one of my books. Not afraid to get out and get a little dirty and especially not afraid of guys.*

"So, what brought you on this trip?" The one named Annette asked.

"Oh, well, I've never been camping before," Hazel said softly. "I wanted to kind of step out of my comfort zone a little."

The girls nodded. "That's cool," Mallory said.

"What about you two?" Hazel asked in return.

The girls looked at each other conspiratorially and broke into laughter. Mallory did a quick glance to the front of the group before curving into Hazel so their words wouldn't be heard. "Turns out both of us just wanted to see Nelson Truman." She giggled. "We've both been camping before and thought maybe we could get to know him." She turned back to Annette. "May the best woman win," she teased, holding out her hand.

A prick of jealousy hit Hazel, and she quickly pushed it away. *It's not like I have any hold over him. So what if he's been nice to me? He's the one in charge, of course he's going to be nice. But he'd never look twice at me otherwise. These two are probably exactly the type of woman he's look-ing for.* The thought made Hazel incredibly sad, but she did her best to ignore the emotion and focus on the other ladies.

Annette leaned around Mallory. "Although, those other two guys aren't too bad looking either." She jabbed her thumb behind her and Hazel turned to see she was talking about Jack and the man he was with.

Hazel swallowed hard. "Uh yeah, not too bad at all." *You can have him.* She stayed silent while the other two women chatted the last cou-ple of minutes until they reached the lake. Hazel skidded to a stop when the water finally came into view. "Whoa..." she whispered.

Bright blue water stood in stark contrast to the deep green of the surrounding forest. Birds flew through the almost cloudless sky and the mountain they were standing on rose higher on her right, creating the perfect backdrop for the scene.

Hazel closed her eyes for a moment and took a deep breath in through her nose. "Mmmm..." she hummed. *Why have I never done this before?*

She suddenly stumbled to the side as someone rammed into her shoulder. "Oh!" She looked over at a grinning Jack.

"You gonna swim or what?" he asked with a pump of his eyebrows.

"N-no thanks," Hazel murmured. Putting her head down, she started to step away.

"Now, wait a minute." Jack reached out and grabbed her arm. "I'm just trying to get to know you. Don't give me the brush off."

Hazel's arm burned where he touched, and not in the pleasant way she had experienced with Nelson. She wanted to tell him to let go of her, but her shy side had taken over and the words died on her lips. Instead, fear made her mouth dry and her heart pick up speed.

"Come on, Sweetheart." He tugged her closer.

Hazel's jaw clamped, and she dug in her heels, but his strength far outdid her own. She raised a hand and pushed it against his chest as he pulled her in.

"I'm not such a bad guy. Give me a chance." One side of his mouth rose in a grin. "We've got a whole week together. You might end up liking me."

Hazel shook her head. *How the heck do I get out of this? Say something!* She pushed again on his chest, but he refused to give up his grip.

"Hey, Dude. Let her go, huh?"

Hazel nearly closed her eyes as feelings of relief soared through her at Nelson's voice. But it didn't last long when Jack actually tightened his grip.

"Who asked you? We're just having a little conversation, Rich Boy," Jack sneered.

"Look, we don't want any trouble, but it's obvious the lady is uncomfortable. Let her go and go cool off."

Hazel could feel Nelson's presence at her back. The hairs on the back of her neck stood on end and every part of her body screamed to move towards him and away from the guy who was holding her captive.

Jack scoffed, but gave her a little shove backward.

Hazel stumbled a little at the sudden release, until Nelson's hands caught her and kept her upright. Her body hummed in agreement with his touch. *Good grief. This crush is getting out of hand.*

"Look, Man, no harm done." Jack gave a grin that was more like a leer. "Guess I'll just chat with you later, Hazel." Adding extra swagger to his step, he walked toward the edge of the lake where his tentmate and the other girls were setting up their chairs and towels.

As the adrenaline from the situation began dissipate in Hazel's body, she felt her limbs begin to tremble.

"Whoa there," Nelson said softly as he felt her shaking. He turned her to face him and she nearly drowned in his concerned gaze. His eyes darted toward the shoreline then back. "Come on," he tilted his head toward the woods.

Like an obedient child, Hazel took the hand he offered and followed behind him. By the time they got out of the sight of the rest of the campers, her teeth were chattering so hard she thought they might break. *Oh my word. Oh my word. Breathe, Hazel. Just breathe and calm down.*

Nelson finally stopped and ducked down so he could look her straight in the eye. "Are you okay?"

"Y-yeah," she stammered, nodding quickly.

"You don't look okay." Nelson scrunched up one side of his face. "Can I- Can I hug you? I don't want to make you feel uncomfortable, but I don't know what else to offer."

Hazel felt some of her tension immediately release at his sweet gesture. Nodding again, she allowed him to wrap his arms around her and tuck her under his chin. She sighed in contentment as she turned her head so her cheek lay against his chest and the heat of his body soothed her frayed nerves. *This must be what heaven is like.*

His hands ran up and down her back, like a parent soothing a child and Hazel revelled in every moment of it. She allowed her eyelids to flutter closed and nearly fell asleep on her feet.

"Feeling better?" His deep voice rumbled through his chest and the sensation only heightened Hazel's awareness of him.

"Yes, thank you," she said softly. *But I don't want to move. You're like one of my book heroes come to life and it's amazing.* She let herself fantasize a little longer and lifted her head so she could look in his eyes. *If we were in a book, we'd kiss right now. The moment would be soft and sticky, maybe a butterfly would fly over our heads adding to the magic...* She could just picture the whole thing.

But instead of her dreams coming true, a crashing through the bushes caught their attention instead.

"Huh," Jack grunted, folding his arms. "So this is why you weren't interested? All this time you've been with him?" He glared at Nelson then at Hazel.

Hazel's jaw dropped and her eyes widened. Once again she was frozen. *He thinks Nelson and I are together?*

To her horror, Nelson pulled her in even tighter and smiled tightly. "Yep. I'm sure you can understand why we felt the need to keep our relationship a secret. Media and all that." Nelson huffed. "They never leave us in peace."

Jack rolled his eyes. "Whatever. You should have said something," he growled, "rather than leading me on."

Hazel's jaw started flapping. "I didn't... I mean we're not... I-I-"

Nelson gave her a little squeeze which caused her to stop talking. Giving her a wink, he stepped back and turned to Jack, folding his arms over his chest. "I think you need to back off, Man. From what I've seen, you've been chasing Hazel like a puppy dog, without any encouragement at all." He shook his head. "She hasn't done anything to lead you on and you know it."

Hazel's eyes darted back and forth between the two men and she knew her face was pale at this latest development. *Why is Nelson saying this? He knows we're not together. I hate lying and I'm terrible at it. The world has gone crazy!*

Jack's hands clenched and he glared at Nelson. "Figures the *rich* guy would get the girl," Jack retorted. "Women never could resist money." He shook his head and scowled at Hazel. "I'm outta here." Turning around, he stormed back through the trees toward the lake.

His leaving finally snapped Hazel out of her stupor. Stepping back, she wrapped her arms around herself to ward off the sudden loss of warmth.

"What in the world was that?" she shouted.

NELSON'S EYEBROWS SHOT up his forehead. *Whoa. I didn't know she had that kind of volume in her.* "Uh, it was me saving you from the jerk." He rubbed the back of his neck. Truth be told, he wasn't sure why he had blurted out that they were dating. It was against everything he had planned for his life right now, but Jack's snotty attitude and his treatment of Hazel finally came to a head when Jack had walked in on their little moment in the woods.

Holding Hazel had felt amazing. When she had agreed to let him hug her, he hadn't thought it would be so perfect. She fit right under his chin and when she had sighed and melted into the embrace, it had sent his pulse skyrocketing. He had forced himself to keep his hands moving on her back, but he had been tempted to do much more.

Then she'd leaned back and he'd looked into her stunning blue eyes and the very air around them had stilled. He could barely breathe and just as he was getting ready to lean down and kiss her, Jack had interrupted.

"Saving me from the jerk?" Hazel put her hands on top of her head and walked around a little.

Nelson pinched his lips between his teeth to keep from laughing at her indignant response. She was so sweet and quiet and seeing her all worked up was like watching an angry kitten.

"I came up here to get out of my comfort zone, not to suddenly gain a fake boyfriend!" she muttered as she paced. "I mean... I know I told him I had a boyfriend at the restaurant last night, but I was just trying to get him to leave me alone! I assumed I would never see him again. Of all the... I'm a terrible liar! Not to mention this is wrong. Just plain wrong." She stopped and looked toward the lake. "He's probably told the whole group by now." She dropped her head backward and groaned. "I'm just going to have to tell them. I can't do this." She took a step toward the lake and Nelson panicked.

"Hey, hey, hey.." He reached out and grabbed her around the waist, pulling her into his body. "Hang on a second, huh? I think maybe we should just let this ride. It solves a lot of problems. Especially if you already told him you were taken, this makes it perfect."

"What? Why would this solve problems? Doesn't it just create them?" Hazel asked in a soft voice as she looked over her shoulder.

"Like, uh..." Nelson's mind had gone blank at being so close to her again, but when she blinked, he shook his head. *Dude! No girls! At least not just one girl! Knock it off!* "Like the fact that now Jack won't hit on you all the time."

"Yeah, but now he thinks I'm a liar who strung him along." Hazel frowned.

Nelson shrugged and let go. He couldn't think straight while he was touching her. "Maybe so, but we know that's not true. He was just embarrassed and threw that out."

"But by doing this, I am a liar. I might not have strung him along, but I'm still lying." She pinched her lips together. "And what other problem does it solve?"

Nelson felt his cheeks heat. "Well, see, it uh." He rubbed the back of his neck. "I heard the girls talking earlier about trying to get me alone."

"The girls?"

"Yeah, uh, Mallory and Annette? They were making bets about who could get me alone first?" He dug his toe in the dirt.

Hazel's eyebrows shot up, and she started to giggle. Her hand came up, and she covered her mouth, but the giggling continued. "They were taking bets? Who does that?"

"You'd be surprised what people will do when someone has money," Nelson said ruefully.

Hazel stopped laughing and concern crossed her face. "I'm sorry. I'm sure that has to be hard. Not knowing who wants you for you and who wants you for your money." She squished her lips to the side. "But, I have to admit that still surprises me." She glanced up at Nelson from under her eyelashes. "I would have expected you to welcome the attentions of girls like that. They're both very pretty and bubbly."

Most of the time I would. "Yeah, well, you said it. *Girls.* I'm not a fan of tiny, little things barely out of high school," Nelson mock whispered.

"Huh. Good to know." Hazel turned to look toward the lake. "We probably ought to head back. I'm not really sure about this. I mean, yeah, I want Jack to leave me alone and it sounds like you're having similar problems, but I really hate lying. Plus, I don't know that anyone is actually going to believe that we're together."

Nelson frowned. "Why wouldn't they?"

Hazel blushed fiercely. "Well, because, I mean... well, you're *you,* and I'm *me.*" She looked at him expectantly as if those convoluted words should explain everything.

"I still don't get it."

Hazel shook her head. "Never mind. Come on." She started walking back out of the woods and without overthinking it, Nelson hurried to catch up, grabbing her hand.

When she looked up at him, startled, he hurried to explain. "It will be more believable if we're holding hands."

"Oh, yeah. I guess so," she responded in a soft voice.

Nelson found himself feeling guilty. *I really shouldn't rope her into this, but what else was I supposed to do? Jack wouldn't leave her alone and I'm definitely not desperate enough to hang out with teenagers. This solves everything. And when we get back to civilization, we'll just have a mutually agreed upon 'break-up' and go our separate ways. No harm done.*

Nodding at his internal pep talk, Nelson plastered a wide smile on his face as he and Hazel came into view of the group. The campers had put towels and blankets on the ground and most were sitting around the water's edge talking and laughing. A few had braved the frigid temperatures by sticking their toes in the water, only to follow the action with squeals and cries of how cold it was.

As they approached, several sets of eyes focused on the two of them. Nelson noticed a couple of his workers smirk in his direction and he chose to ignore their knowing expressions. However, he carefully kept an eye on Jack and the girls to see what they would do.

Jack's face still showed displeasure, but he made no move to approach him and Hazel. The girls glanced at his and Hazel's hands and their faces simultaneously broke into surprise, followed by pouts.

It's a wonder they didn't know each other before they came. They are definitely two of a kind.

Annette leaned in and said something to Mallory who nodded and shrugged. Then the girls both went back to lounging in the sun.

Hopefully, that's the end of that.

Hazel's grip went slack and Nelson let her pull away.

"I should probably go sit with the girls. They were being very nice to me on the walk over here," she whispered.

"Yeah. I should go make sure everyone has what they need. I'll check on you later," Nelson said in return.

Her eyebrows slashed down. "Why-" she started before snapping her mouth shut. "Oh, yeah. Gotta make it look good." She smiled, but it looked strained. "Got it." Turning, Hazel walked over to where her backpack had dropped when Jack had grabbed her. She then went to go sit by the girls, who immediately accosted her with a dozen questions.

Nelson chose not to wonder why he waited to make sure she was doing alright before he went about his duties. He chose not to wonder why he kept checking on her every few minutes the rest of the after-noon. He also chose not to wonder why he didn't like having her so far away from him. Instead, he chose to act as a helpful host, making sure everyone was comfortable and followed the rules of the group. But when he went to bed that night, he couldn't help but wonder when he would get the chance to hold Hazel in his arms again. *But just because I'm trying to convince the group we're a couple. That's all.*

CHAPTER 6

Hazel woke the next morning to the raucous sound of a thousand birds. Moaning, she rolled over. "Oh my gosh. I thought birds were supposed to be soothing and sweet. It sounds like they're trying to kill something out there!"

When the noise didn't die down, she gave up and poked her head out of the plush sleeping bag. "Oh!" With a shiver, she pulled herself back in. "What temperature is it?" She rubbed her nose which felt like ice and frowned. "It's summertime. Why in the world is it so cold?"

As she sat contemplating how to handle the situation, her bladder let her know that she better make up her mind soon. With a growl, Hazel jumped out of her bag, grabbed her sweatshirt and socks, and headed toward the front of the tent. Jamming her feet in her shoes, she stepped into the crisp morning air.

"Oooh...." She shivered and hugged herself. Glancing around, she noticed very few people had stirred yet. With a quick glance around the campsite, she darted into the woods to the place they had designated as a 'private zone'. After taking care of business, she walked back to the tents.

Stepping out of the woods and into a patch of morning sunlight, she sighed and closed her eyes in enjoyment. *Soooo much better. How can there be such a difference between the shadows and the sun? Good heavens.*

She opened her eyes when she heard chuckling. She met Nelson's dark ones, and she nearly sighed again.

Nelson lips twitched as if he was fighting the smile stretched across his face, but he had obviously lost the battle. "Hot chocolate?" He held up a mug in her direction.

"Yes, please." Hazel returned his smile at her expense and walked toward him and the fire.

Hazel grabbed the tin mug with both hands and soaked in the warmth she found there. Tentatively she took a sip. "Ooh, it's too hot."

Nelson nodded. "Yeah. The water just came off the fire." He stepped back toward a fallen log. "Come on, have a seat." He patted the spot next to him.

Hazel followed but made sure there was a little distance between them. *I already had a crush on him and if he keeps up this fake relationship thing, I'm gonna be in real trouble.*

"Sleep good?" Nelson took a sip of his own mug.

"Yeah, actually." Hazel gave a small smile and glanced at him before looking back down at her mug. "I thought the night noises might keep me up, but I was exhausted apparently, because I slept great until the bird mob woke me up."

Nelson choked on his drink and coughed a couple of times. His face was bright red by the time he got a good breath. "Bird mob?" He rasped out, hitting his chest a couple of times.

"Uh, yeah. You always read in books that the sounds of nature in the morning are wonderful and sweet. Well, apparently none of those authors have ever slept in a real forest because I thought it sounded like a choir of dying ghouls this morning."

Nelson was cracking up beside her and Hazel felt a stirring of warmth that she had made him laugh. "That's quite the description." He took another drink. "You read a lot then?"

Hazel shrugged. "Yeah. I suppose so."

Nelson dropped his voice and leaned in close to her ear. "What do you do for work? That's probably something I should know if we're going to pull this off, right?"

Crud. This is where I lose people. "I, uh, I'm a writer."

Nelson paused and grinned. "A writer? Really?"

Hazel felt her defenses rising. She didn't get upset very often, but almost every time she spoke about her profession, the other person would make derogatory comments about the fact that she wrote romance. "Yes. A writer," she snipped.

Nelson's eyebrows shot up at her tone.

Calm down, Hazel, he hasn't actually said anything wrong.

"That's cool. What do you write?"

Hazel paused with her mouth open. She hadn't been expecting his easy acceptance. "Umm... romance."

Nelson grinned. "I should have known."

"What's that supposed to mean?" She asked before she could think better of it. *I probably don't want to know what he meant by that.*

Nelson shrugged. "You're just so sweet and innocent. I can totally see you writing happy ever afters for the people in your books."

A slow smile crawled across her face. "That's probably one of the nicest things anyone has ever said to me," she said softly. "Most people think what I do is a waste of time." *He really would be the best book boyfriend of all time.*

Nelson poked a stick at the fire. "Well, if it's what you enjoy, who cares what anyone else thinks? My brothers think I play for a living, so..." He shrugged.

Hazel frowned. *Why does he sound so sad about that?* "I think most people would love the chance to play for a living. I don't see anything wrong with it."

Nelson gave her a grateful smile. "Thanks. I love what I do. I couldn't handle being shut up in an office all day." He gave an exaggerated shiver.

Hazel laughed lightly before finishing her hot chocolate. Glancing up from their conversation, she realized most of the campers were up and gathered around the fire and staring at her and Nelson. Her cheeks heated, and she ducked her head.

"Looks like it's time to get this party started," Nelson said into her ear. Slapping a hand on her knee, he stood and said good morning before telling everyone the options for breakfast.

Hazel continued to sit on the log, unable to make herself move from the spot where she had just shared a wonderful conversation with a wonderful man. She logged every detail she could think of into her memory so she could put the thoughts onto paper when she had a chance. And if the tingling sensation on her knee from his touch was one of those memories, so much the better.

NELSON HELPED HIS CREW set out the breakfast they had brought up with them. Today they were having the fancy options. Daniel was scrambling eggs, and Jerome was showing everyone how to make pancakes over the fire. Nelson started unpacking the fruit and the rest of the hot chocolate packets.

He'd been pleasantly surprised when he'd seen Hazel emerge from her tent before most of the other campers, but then he'd had a fleeting worry that maybe she hadn't slept well and that's why she was up so early.

Her disgruntlement had been adorable when she'd been complaining about the horrible chorus of birds waking her up. Nelson grinned to himself. *They were pretty loud this morning, but it's all just part of the package of being outdoors.*

Over the years, he had gotten used to the noises in the forest and didn't think anything of them any more. But he had enjoyed listening to Hazel and learning what she did for work. He thought about how she told him she wrote romances. *Considering she's so quiet and shy, a writer is probably the perfect job for her. She works on her own and doesn't have to deal with other people very often. But then, what brought her on this trip?*

He glanced over to where she sat with Mallory and Annette. The two younger girls were chatting a mile a minute while Hazel simply smiled and nodded. He found he liked that about her. She was kind, and she didn't stay away from people just because she was quieter than they were. *Not that there's much choice out here. She's kinda stuck. Speaking of stuck...* Nelson glanced around to see where Jack was. He and Tyler, his tentmate were eating a plate full of pancakes and eggs while they both eyed the girls. *Hmm... I'll have to keep an eye on things. Hopefully, those two don't start causing problems with the other girls now.*

As people started finishing their breakfasts, Nelson instructed his crew to start putting the supplies away. "Jerome and I will start prepping for the hike if you guys will get breakfast put away."

Everyone nodded and split in different directions.

Nelson walked up to the fire and raised his hands. "Hey, everyone!" He smiled. "Hope you all slept good last night because you're gonna need the energy today! Today's activity is a five-mile hike. We'll be going uphill for the first half and there will be a surprise at the turnaround point."

The group murmured softly as he spoke.

"Lucky for us, the sun is supposed to stay shining today. So I would encourage you to not only put on your sunscreen but also bring some with you. Hats are a good idea, along with your good solid footwear. No sandals, please. If you have bug repellant, I would plan on using it. Especially since we'll be going through a couple of dense areas and we really don't want anyone to pick up a tick or anything."

Nelson noticed Hazel's eyes widen and her face pale. *Wow. She really is a newbie. Guess I'll just have to help her.* He thought smugly.

"If you brought a swimsuit, feel free to wear it under your clothes. Any questions?" He looked around, but nobody seemed concerned with his directions except for Hazel.

"Ready? Break!"

Small bits of laughter drifted to him as the group went back to their tents to gather their supplies.

"Should we grab the picnic stuff?" Nelson asked Daniel, who was standing just behind his shoulder.

"On it, Boss," Daniel replied. "Perhaps you should go help your little lady friend with her packing, huh?" He winked and started to walk away.

"We're not-" Nelson stopped himself. *Oh... yeah we are. Or at least we want people to think we are.* "That's a good idea!" Nelson said with a smile. He ignored Daniel's guffaw and sauntered over to Hazel's tent.

The opening was unzipped and he could see her squatting down next to her bed.

"Need any help in there?" he called in.

She jerked then looked at him. "Oh, no. At least I don't think so. I'm fine."

Nelson crouched down and moved the flap aside so he could see her better. "Show me what you have in your pack," he said softly.

Hazel scrunched up her nose. "I followed your online directions to the letter, so I should have everything you said we need."

Nelson took the backpack she offered and looked inside. Granola bars, bug spray, bear spray, a light sweatshirt and a couple of water bottles were thrown in. Looking up, he froze for a second when he realized how close they were to each other. She had leaned in to look inside as well and her wide, blue eyes were doing something to him. "S-sunscreen?" He finally managed to ask. Without conscious thought, one of his hands went up to her cheek and stroked the soft skin there. "We wouldn't want you to get burnt today. Especially since we're at a higher altitude than you're used to."

That creamy skin flushed bright pink and Nelson yanked his hand back before he could do something else foolish. *Like kiss her.*

"Yeah. It's in the outer pocket." She shrugged. "I can't leave home without it."

Nelson nodded. "I can see why." His eyes continued to study her face before he cleared his throat and backed up. Standing, he offered the backpack to her. "Looks good. You probably should stay close to me today. You know," he dropped his voice and looked around, "so we come across as a couple and all."

Her cheeks were still fiery pink and she wouldn't look him in the eye. "Yeah. Good idea. Thanks."

"'Kay, see ya in a bit." Nelson forced his feet to move and go back to check on the other campers. *Dude! What is wrong with you? This is fake. You only need to convince the people in the camp you're together so that Jack will leave her alone. Nothing else. Remember, this is your time to shine.*

Thirty minutes later Nelson stood in the front of the group waving his arm to get everyone's attention. "Is everyone ready?" He shouted.

A chorus of yeses came back at him and Nelson grinned. "Great. Remember to stay together, there will lots of things to see and I will do my best to make sure you get to see them. If you have questions, ask. If you're not sure what something is, don't touch it!" He dropped his voice dramatically and several chuckles came from the crowd. "Okay, here we go! Off to Neverland!"

More laughter followed him as he turned and started walking. Glancing over his shoulder, he caught Hazel's eye. With a tilt of his chin, he invited her to come walk beside him.

He grinned as her cheeks turned pink and she excused herself from the little girl she had been walking next to.

"Looks like you made a friend," Nelson said with a smirk.

Hazel looked back and waved at the child. "Yeah. She's pretty sweet." Hazel turned to look at Nelson and mischief twinkled in her eyes. "She wanted to ask me if you were really my boyfriend."

Nelson's eyebrows shot up. "She did?"

"Yeah. She was very disappointed to find out you weren't available at the moment. But then she told me it was okay, because I was pretty."

Nelson snorted. "Wow. I can't say I've ever caught the eye of anyone quite so young before. Her parents are going to have their hands full if this is how she is at age five."

Hazel rolled her eyes and whacked his arm. "She's ten, Nelson."

"Oh." He cleared his throat. "Sorry."

Hazel laughed lightly. "That's alright. I won't tell her you thought she was a kindergartner."

"Thanks. I wouldn't want her coming after me with a roasting stick or anything."

Hazel smiled and shook her head. "So... what are we going to see on this hike?"

Now it was Nelson's turn to smile and shake his head. "Nuh-uh. I said it was a surprise. Don't think you get special girlfriend privileges or anything."

Hazel pursed her lips and narrowed her eyes. "Well, then don't expect any special boyfriend privileges."

"What? Boyfriends always get special privileges." Nelson put his hand on his chest in mock horror.

"Oh really?" Hazel raised an eyebrow. "I create boyfriends. Believe me, they don't get any special privileges."

"Well, then you need to do better research. Tell you what..." Nelson made a point of looking around before ducking his head close to hers. "You can use me as research for your next book." His grin widened. "I give you permission to experiment all you want."

Hazel jolted and her eyes went wide.

Uh, oh. Too much?

"Wow..." Hazel turned her eyes toward the ground. "That's quite the offer. Thanks."

Nelson frowned. "Uh... that's not quite the response I was expecting."

Her eyes darted up before going back to the ground. "Just what *were* you expecting when you tell a girl you don't think she has any romantic experience?"

Nelson opened his mouth to speak, then paused. "Oh. I didn't realize that's how it sounded. Shoot." He rubbed the back of his neck. "Maybe I'm not a good guy to research on after all."

Hazel blurted out a loud laugh. "I know you didn't mean it that way, but that's how it sounded to my girl-brain."

"Girl-brain?" Nelson scrunched up his nose. "Do I want to know what that is?"

Hazel stuck her nose in the air. "You don't *get* to know what that is. Women are a mystery to men for a reason."

Nelson rolled his eyes. "That's so dumb. If we understood you, it would be way easier to make sure we didn't hurt your feelings."

"Yeah, but it would also be way easier to get your way by manipulating our feelings," Hazel pointed a finger at him.

Nelson grinned.

Hazel threw up her hands. "Which is exactly what you want, isn't it? See... if I was writing this scene, this is not where this would have gone."

Nelson's interest was peaked. Before talking again, he looked back to see how the crowd was doing and so far, it all looked fine. *Early days yet, Nelson. Early days.* "So tell me, oh wonderful author... how would you have written it?"

Hazel pinched her lips together as she thought. "Well, first of all, you would have called me by a cute nickname. You know, one that showed how you felt about me."

"Like what? Honey? Sweetie Pie? Cutesy wootsy?"

"Ugh," Hazel shook her head and laughed. "Not even. Like beautiful girl, my love or one that I cannot live without."

"It's a wonder your books sell," Nelson mumbled teasingly.

"Oooh, you!" She smacked him on the arm again, but her smile let him know she wasn't really upset.

"Hey! In a romance the girl wouldn't whack the guy so much." He rubbed his arm. "It could be considered boyfriend abuse."

Hazel rolled her eyes. "Baby."

"I prefer sensitive," Nelson corrected. "Isn't that what girls like? A sensitive man?"

"Sensitive with his feelings, not one that can't take a little tap on the arm!" Hazel said incredulously.

"You call that a tap? Where do you-"

"Trouble in paradise?" Jack walked up on Hazel's other side and grinned obnoxiously at Nelson before turning to look at Hazel, who had gone quiet.

"No," Nelson stated bluntly, wrapping his arm around Hazel's shoulder and tucking her into his side as they walked. "We were just having a friendly discussion."

"Didn't sound very friendly," Jack said snidely. "In fact, it sounded like two people who don't really get along." Jack reached out and ran his hand up Hazel's arm, causing her to jerk further into Nelson's side. "Maybe you should come give someone else a chance, Sweetheart."

Nelson clenched his jaw to keep from saying something his mother would have washed out his mouth for. *Who does he think he is? And why the heck won't he leave her alone? Anyone can see she's not interested, even if we weren't pretending to be together.*

"No thanks," Hazel said softly.

"Look, man, I don't know who you think you are, but she's not available. Just leave her alone." Nelson's voice was quiet, but deadly.

Jack glared right back. "You know what? I don't think you two are really together. I think you've bullied her into this. You with all your money and your high and mighty attitude. Well, let me tell you something, Mr. Billionaire." Jack leaned in closer. "I. Don't. Lose." After that parting shot, Jack dropped back and began hiking with the other single campers.

Nelson was seeing red. *If I get that guy alone, I'm gonna-*

Hazel stood, straightening from where she had been tucked under his arm. "Maybe we should just tell the truth," she whispered, glancing nervously over her shoulder. "I don't know why he picked me out in the first place, but it's obvious right now it's not about me, it's more a matter of pride."

"Not a chance," Nelson said through his clenched jaw. "Hang on a sec." Reaching out, he took her hand and sped up just a bit. After a minute, he pulled her to the side of the trail as he turned back to the crowd. "Alrighty, folks! You've all been doing great! Here is our first rest and our first view. Feel free to have a seat on any of the fallen logs, but keep an eye out for ants and termites. Get a good drink, take a few pictures of the valley and in about ten minutes, we'll continue on our way."

Shouts of delight and the groans of weary walkers echoed through the air as a good portion of the group dropped to the ground. Zippers could be heard as everyone grabbed their water bottles to take a hearty gulp.

"Come with me," Nelson said quietly. Keeping a hold of Hazel's hand, he ducked into a stand of trees.

"Whoa..." Hazel looked around the little grove. Even though it was right next to the trail, the branches of the trees muted the outside sounds and it seemed as if they were in their own little world. "I feel like fairies or gnomes are going to come crawling out of the bushes any second."

Nelson huffed a laugh before folding his arms. "We need to do something about that guy."

Hazel shrugged and studied her shoe. "I don't know what we can do. He's a jerk, obviously. His pride is hurt, and he's lashing out."

Nelson shook his head. "What are you? Some kind of psychologist?"

Hazel glanced up and grinned. "No. I'm a writer."

Nelson chuckled. "But seriously, though. The dude is an adult and has no right to be so rude. I want you to make sure you stay close to me, okay? I don't trust him to not hurt you."

Hazel jerked her head up, her eyes wide and frightened. "You really think he'd hurt me?"

Nelson took off his hat and ran his hands through his hair. "Well, I hope not, but seriously, with that challenge he threw down, I don't know for sure. We're just going to have to up our game. Hopefully, when he finally believes we're together, he'll back off." *Like the loser he is.* Nelson held in his last thought, deciding Hazel probably wouldn't like the smugness.

"What exactly does 'upping our game' entail?" she asked warily.

Kissing you. Nelson also kept that thought to himself, although he knew he wouldn't object to it in the slightest. *Focus, Nelson.* "Just staying close, holding hands, you know. That kind of thing."

She wiggled her lips from side to side for a moment and Nelson found himself holding his breath. *Why am I so worried about this? I'm not looking to settle down. This is just to keep her safe from jerkface until we get done with this camping trip.*

Hazel nodded and stuck her chin in the air. "Okay. Thank you. I'm really grateful for your intervention with him. He's pretty aggressive and I have a hard time saying 'no.'"

"Shocker," Nelson said blandly.

"Well, some of us only write our sarcasm. We don't actually say it out loud."

Nelson grinned and held out his hand. "Well, then come on little Lady Love. We have convincing to do."

"That nickname will definitely not be a way to do it," Hazel groaned.

Nelson laughed and pulled her back to the trail and the waiting campers.

CHAPTER 7

Hazel found herself huffing and puffing as they climbed the last bit of the hike before the turn around point. She could tell her cheeks were as red as ripe tomatoes as she sucked in the life giving oxygen to her underfed lungs.

Sweat trickled down her back and she refused to look down to see if her shirt was sticking to her. *I don't want to know what I look like or what I smell like.*

"You doing okay?" Nelson asked with a frown. "We're almost there, but you're really red." He studied her closer. "Have you been drinking water?"

Hazel nodded. "Enough to drown an elephant," she huffed.

Nelson's lip twitched and Hazel fought the desire to grin back at him. "This surprise had better be worth it. I'm going to have to gorge on an entire package of Oreos to make up for this hike."

Nelson blurted out a laugh that was loud enough to scare a few birds from the nests. "Dang, Girl. You need to warn me before you bring out the snark. It's awesome."

Hazel thought she might burst into flames. Now her cheeks were flaming from embarrassment as well as hiking.

Nelson leaned in close and Hazel couldn't help but take a big breath of his earthy scent. *He smells like pine trees. How the heck does he smell so good when I must stink like a dead skunk? Sooooo unfair.*

"I promise it will be worth it." Nelson's words penetrated through her pine-scented fog and finally registered.

"Oh, good. Great. I can't wait," she stammered out.

"In fact," Nelson gave a grin that made Hazel want to swoon, "we're here."

Hazel's eyes shot to where Nelson waved his arm and frowned. "I don't see anything."

Nelson had stopped walking. Pumping his eyebrows, he turned back to the group. "Surprise!" He raised his arms in the air.

Everyone looked around, but they were just as confused as Hazel.

Nelson put his finger to his lips. "Shhhh.... Listen closely and see if you can figure it out."

The entire group closed their mouths and listened. At first, the only thing Hazel could hear was those noisy birds who never seemed to shut up, but the longer she concentrated, the more acute her ears became. Soon she could make out the buzzing of insects and just beyond that was a sound that caught her interest. She gasped and turned to Nelson. "I hear water!"

"Me too!"

"Where is it?"

The whole group began talking excitedly, their lagging energy restored at the thought of cool, running water.

Nelson waved his arm. "Come on! Right over this rise." His legs took long, confident strides up the short hill. Hazel had to force her legs to keep moving so she didn't block the flow of traffic.

"Oh my gosh! It's gorgeous!" Her jaw hung slack and her eyes couldn't seem to focus on just one thing. *It's like something out of a fairy tale.* A small waterfall fell into a larger pool area that eventually funneled out into a small river.

"Man, is that deep enough to swim in?" The teenage boy in the group had run up to Nelson's side. He was fumbling with his phone and finally started snapping pictures.

"Yeah." Nelson grinned. "You can even jump off the waterfall if you go straight out. There's a really deep spot in the middle, but the sides are more shallow."

"Mom! Take my picture!" The kid ran off again without responding to Nelson's words.

Hazel laughed. "I think that's the first time I've seen him excited about anything since we got here."

"Truer words have never been spoken." Nelson chuckled. Reaching out he grabbed her hand again.

That dang blush worked its way back up Hazel's cheeks. *Sheesh. I know this is all fake, so why the heck do I still blush every time he touches me?* She internally rolled her eyes. *Because you have a crush on your perfect boyfriend, you idiot.* "Too bad it's not real," she muttered to herself.

"Hmm?" Nelson turned toward her. "Did you say something?"

Hazel pasted a smile on her face. "Nope. Nothing at all."

Nelson gave her a look that said he didn't believe her, but he let it drop. "So, what do you think?" He pulled her in front of him, so she was facing the water and he wrapped his arms around her waist.

That I don't ever want to move out of your arms and I'm going to be in serious trouble when this is all over. "It's gorgeous. I can't believe this is just hiding up here."

Nelson nodded and Hazel felt it against the top of her head. "Yeah. I was pretty surprised when I found it, but it's one of my favorites places. The water is cold enough to turn your blood to sludge, but it's fun anyway. When I get too cold, I just lay out on one of the rocks like a lizard or something until I warm up."

Hazel laughed. "That does not sound fun to me."

Nelson gave her a squeeze, then stepped around her and pulled her forward. "Then you'll just have to try it and find out I'm right."

Hazel dug in her heels. "Uh, no thanks. I'm not really a big swimmer."

Nelson looked back as he continued to pull her forward, a twinkle in his eye. "Oh, you're not just going to swim. You're going to jump."

Hazel froze, fear skittering up her spine at the thought of leaping off a waterfall. "You're joking right? Please tell me you're joking."

Nelson shook his head. "No way. How many times in your life are you going to get this chance? You are absolutely doing it."

"Once. Only once does someone get a chance like this, because after that they're in the hospital with a broken neck and can never jump again."

Nelson bent over with loud laughter. "Haze, you are a riot." He wiped his eyes, and he started pulling her reluctant legs forward again. "I've jumped dozens of times and never had a problem."

"There's a problem with your brain," she muttered. Hazel cringed when Nelson started laughing again, realizing he had heard what she had said. *I need to learn to keep my thoughts to myself or my books. Talking about loud just gets me in trouble.*

"Who's going to be brave and go first?" Nelson shouted to the group.

The group had gone around Nelson and Hazel and everyone was already stripping their outer clothes off and setting up places to relax on the edge of the pool. At Nelson's question, the activity stopped, and they looked around.

Hazel noticed that Jack was eyeing her and he began to grin. Just as he stepped forward to speak, the teen boy jumped in. "I'm on it! Mom! Film it!"

Jack scowled, but didn't say anything and Hazel found herself stifling a giggle at his moment being thwarted.

The lanky boy scrambled up the rocks and began tip toeing out to the center of the waterfall. It was only about fifteen feet high and the water flow was manageable for walking through.

"Careful, Luke," his mother called.

The boy waved her away and looked down at Nelson. "This the right spot?"

Nelson nodded and let go of Hazel to cup his hands around his mouth. "Yeah. Now if you look down, you can see a real dark spot in the water, just past where the waterfall lands."

Luke nodded.

"Jump in that. It's the deepest spot."

Luke glanced at Nelson and then looked back down. Hazel could see him gulp before steeling his nerves. She felt her own muscles tighten anxiously as he worked up his courage. As he leapt, Hazel held her breath until she saw his head pop back up from the water, flinging droplets over the nearby rocks.

"Holy crap that's cold!" Luke shouted before swimming over to the edge where he stood and shook himself like a dog.

The entire group cheered and Luke began bowing and waving his arms.

"Your turn..." Nelson said ominously in her ear.

Hazel kept a fake smile plastered on her face and continued clapping. Out of the corner of her mouth she whispered back, "over my dead body."

Nelson chuckled. "Don't worry, it won't come to that. I'll be with you the whole way."

"Then maybe I should have said, over *your* dead body," she said sweetly, tilting her head and batting her eyelashes.

Nelson laughed again. "I had no idea when we first met that you had such a kick. Where do you hide it?"

Hazel relaxed a little and her smile became more genuine. "My mother would tell you that I don't hide it. In actuality, I usually save it for my books, but being this far out of my comfort zone seems to be bringing out my sassy side."

Nelson pursed his lips and nodded, while slowly winking one eye. "Your secret is safe with me."

"Good to know," Hazel laughed.

"COME ON, HAZE," NELSON encouraged. "Almost there." He bit back a smile as she mumbled under her breath. *I wish I knew what she was saying. She's hilarious when she gets all full of attitude.*

He reached out and offered his hand. Hazel gripped it like a lifeline and Nelson could feel her trembling. For a moment he felt bad about talking her into jumping, but he pushed it aside. *If she really put up a fuss, I'd leave her alone, but I think she wants to try it, she's just too scared to do it on her own.*

"I can't believe I'm doing this," Hazel said through clenched teeth. She stood next to him at the top of the waterfall in her tankini.

Nelson could see goosebumps on her exposed skin, and he scrunched his nose. *If she's cold now, she's going to be frozen when we hit the water.* "Just think of it this way." Nelson grinned flirtatiously. "You'll have something to write about in your next book."

"Yeah, been trying that and I'm still scared stiff. Obviously, it's always good to have first hand knowledge, but I'm thinking more and more that I should just watch a few videos online."

Nelson shook his head and clucked his tongue. "Not the same, Hazey Girl. Not the same. No video can give you an accurate description of what it's like to have a big shot of adrenaline hit you all at once. Or what it's like to conquer a fear."

"Or you know... die," Hazel grimaced.

Nelson pulled her forward and wrapped his arms around her as best he could as they balanced on the rocks. "No one is dying today, Haze. Not on my watch."

Hazel sighed and leaned into his chest a little more and Nelson couldn't help but enjoy the sensation. *No getting attached, Dude. We've had this discussion before.*

"Are you going to jump or what?" Jack's obnoxious tone came from below.

Nelson scowled. "Chill, Man. She's nervous."

"Doesn't look nervous to me. Just looks like you're finding an excuse to touch her."

Hazel leaned away from his chest and ducked her head away from the crowd.

The more Jack talked, the more Nelson found himself wanting to take the guy out. *One roundhouse kick. That's all it would take. One well placed kick.*

"Maybe I should just climb down so I'm not holding up the line anymore," Hazel murmured.

Stupid, Jack. "Nope. You're already here. We're definitely doing this." Nelson said confidently.

"Come on, Hazel! You can do it!" Mallory yelled from below.

"Yep! Come on, Hazel!" Annette joined in.

Nelson smiled in gratitude at the young women. "See? They know you can do it, too. Now, come on. Take my hand." Hazel's fingers were cold, clammy and shaking uncontrollably when she grasped him. "On the count of three, okay?"

She nodded quickly.

"One... two..." With a whoop, Nelson leapt off the rock, taking a screaming Hazel with him. They landed with a splash and he quickly pushed air out his nose to keep from sucking in water.

Once they stopped descending, he pumped his legs and pulled the two of them to the surface. "Whoo!" he yelled as their heads broke through the icy water.

Hazel coughed a couple of times and gulped in large quantities of air, while wiping the water out of her eyes.

"You okay?" Nelson studied her while he kicked his legs, treading water.

Hazel didn't answer him for a moment and he began to feel the first stirring of panic that she had hated their little jump. But then a smile began split her face. "That was awesome! Oh my gosh! I can't believe I did that! Ha ha!" She laughed wildly and flung her hair out of her eyes.

Nelson laughed with her and began to tug her to the side where they could sit for a few minutes.

"Brrrr... that's stinkin' cold," Hazel stuttered as they moved into the shallower water. Her body was shaking as badly as it had been before they jumped, but from the wild grin on her face, Nelson was hoping it was from cold rather than nerves.

"Hey, Hazel!" Jack shouted. "Head right on over here! I'll warm you right up!"

Nelson pinched his lips into a thin, white line and he was grateful when he saw Mallory and Annette come to Hazel's defense. Mallory smacked Jack on the arm and both girls started scolding him.

Huh. Who would have thought they would actually help? He felt bad for thinking the two girls were going to be a handful and promised himself he wouldn't judge a book by its cover anymore. *Ha! A book by its cover. I should tell that one to Hazel.*

Nelson found himself thinking more and more about Hazel. Despite the fact that he had started this relationship with the intention of saving her from Jack, he had slipped into the role of Hazel's boyfriend way too easily. It felt natural to reach for her hand or wrap his arm around her shoulders. He loved listening to her ramblings and when she got worked up and her snark appeared, it made him laugh. He also found he enjoyed showing her how to push her boundaries. Getting her to jump off that small waterfall and seeing her push past her fear had made him want to puff up like a peacock. The obvious trust she had in him was all too addictive. He found himself thinking of all the other things he could show her. All the other adventures they could go on together. *Dude, it's got to stop. This is getting way out of control. You're not looking for a relationship right now. When are you going to get that into your head?*

"You alright?" Hazel tentatively touched his arm and the warmth Nelson was becoming accustomed to filled him.

"Yeah." Nelson grinned. "Sorry. Just drifted off." He used his hand to shake the water out of his hair, making Hazel squeal. "Maybe I didn't get enough sleep last night, you know with those killer birds and all."

Hazel shoulder bumped him as they sat hip to hip. "Jerk. I can't help it I've been lied to my entire life."

"So, what kind of family vacations did you guys take if you never went camping?" Nelson found himself curious about her childhood and growing up.

Hazel smiled. "We actually didn't go on vacations much. Lots of kids, not lots of money. We went to the coastline a couple of times, staying in cheap hotels. But that's about it." She shrugged. "We had what we needed, but I guess you could say we usually did the 'stay-cation' thing. Our summer was filled with swim lessons, epic water balloon fights, homemade slip 'n slides." She laughed and that single dimple appeared. "One time, my mom splurged and bought this massive black tarp. It was like seventy-five feet long. My dad used old bricks to hold it down and hooked up a couple of PVC pipe sprinklers so we could spread water all the way down it. Best. Slide. Ever."

"Whoa... that's crazy!" Nelson grinned. "You must have had a big backyard."

"Yeah. We had about an acre, so it was big enough for all of us. Believe it or not, my parents were big on outside time. We had a large garden and a few chickens. So I've, you know, actually seen the sun before."

Nelson cracked up. "Glad to hear it. That sounds awesome." He rubbed his chin. "Wish we had thought of that. My brothers and I would have loved it."

Hazel grinned. She hung her arms over her bent knees and watched the other campers play in the water.

"So, if you've done a seventy-five foot slide, why in the world did a fifteen foot jump freak you out?"

Hazel tick-tocked her head back and forth. "Well, I haven't done that kiddy stuff in a long time. Not to mention, heights freak me out in general. Not like how some people get. I'm not deathly afraid, but I'm not a fan." She sighed. "I guess I've just gotten too settled in my quiet lifestyle. I live alone, and I write on my computer all day. Doesn't leave a lot of time for adventures." She huffed out a laugh. "Plus, if you promise not to tell my parents, I'll let you in on a little secret." She turned her large, blue eyes up at Nelson and he had to hold in the urge to say he would promise her anything if she would just keep looking at him.

Snap out of it! He cleared his throat and forced an answering grin on his face. "Since I don't know your parents, I would say that's a pretty safe promise to make."

"True... true." Hazel nodded. "Well, you can probably guess that I was a bit of a book worm growing up, you know, being a writer and all."

Nelson nodded.

"There were way too many times when I was supposed to be playing outside, and instead I snuck up into the treehouse with a book and read away the afternoon."

Nelson waited, but that seemed to be the end of her story. "Uh... is that it? That's your big secret?"

Hazel pushed her bottom lip out in a pout. "Uh, yeah! I just told you one of my deepest, darkest secrets and you mock me? I'll have you know I felt like quite the rebel at the time. If my mother had found me, she would have taken my book and made me work in the garden or something."

Nelson's face was completely emotionless. "That is the lamest rebellion story I have ever heard."

"Hey!" Hazel laughed and shoulder bumped him again. "Why don't you tell my your biggest rebellion story then, huh? You talk the talk but can you walk the walk?"

"You really wanna hear it?" Nelson raised an eyebrow. "I'm worried you won't be able to handle hearing about the awesomeness that is Nelson Truman."

Hazel laughed hard and her whole face lit up. The sight of her joy sent that warmth through Nelson's chest again and he had to ignore the urge to rub the sensation. *What is it about this girl? She's sweet and fragile, basically my exact opposite, and yet something as dumb as being the reason she laughs makes me feel like I've won the Olympics.*

"I await your story, Oh Rebellious King. Lay it on me."

Nelson opened his mouth just as Luke landed in the water yet again.

Hazel squealed and laughed, raising her arms in the air as if her hands could hold off the splash.

Normally, Nelson would have laughed right along with her and then given Luke a hard time. Instead, he felt frustrated at having Hazel's attention taken from him. *Platonic, Dude. This is fake.* But no matter how many times he reminded himself of that fact, he knew he was in trouble. This sweet, little romance author was under his skin and he wasn't sure how to change that. Or if he even truly wanted to.

CHAPTER 8

Hazel limped out of her tent that evening, holding in her groans with every footstep. Not only were her calves and thighs already sore from the day's hike, but she had a couple of big blisters on the back of her heels from her brand new hiking boots. They had started to rub hard on the trip back down the mountain, but Hazel hadn't said anything. *No one likes a whiny girl. Especially not someone like Nelson Truman.*

Once back at her tent, Hazel had carefully taken off her shoes and examined her feet. "Good thing I brought bandages," she grumbled. Biting her lip to keep from whimpering, Hazel did her best to dress her feet.

Once done, she plopped back on her sleeping bag, thoroughly exhausted. Letting her eyes flutter closed, she thought back on the day's events. Jumping off the waterfall had been a first for her and she was proud of herself for following Nelson's lead. "What girl wouldn't go anywhere he asked?" she mumbled under her breath. "I think I'd follow Nelson Truman right off a cliff."

"Hey," Nelson's deep voice penetrated through her nylon walls.

Hazel gasped and jerked to an upright position. *Please say he didn't hear what I just said.* "Uh... hey," Hazel called back.

"Can I come in?" Nelson scratched at her tent.

"Sure," she cleared her throat and ran a hand over her hair. *Ugh, I probably have the world's worst hat hair. Just my luck.*

The tent door unzipped and Nelson poked his head in. "How ya doing?" He grinned and Hazel felt her heart pick up speed.

Fake! This is all fake, Sister! Don't let him get to you! But despite her best scolding, Hazel knew she was in trouble. With every touch, look and word that came from the handsome billionaire, she felt herself fall a little more.

"I-I'm all right. Thanks. How are you?" Hazel mentally slapped her hand to her forehead. *Could I have sounded any more dumb? I'm a writer for heaven's sake! It shouldn't be that hard to come up with something witty. I do it all the time with my characters.*

"Just fine, thanks…" His voice trailed off as his eyes went to her feet. "What happened?" He frowned and fell onto his knees so he could crawl inside her tent.

Hazel nearly jumped out of her skin when Nelson reached out and grabbed one of her ankles to look at her feet. *Awww, geez. My feet probably stink and he's holding them!* She tried to pull her foot out of his grasp, but he ignored her tugs. "Uh… haha, you know…" She laughed uncomfortably. "Just a few blisters from the hike."

Nelson's dark eyes met her. "Weren't you wearing socks?"

"Well, yeah, but all of my stuff is brand new. My boots were pretty stiff and my socks were a little scratchy. They've only been washed once."

His eyebrows scrunched even further. "We're doing a little more exploring tomorrow." He squished his lips to one side. "We're going to have to figure out something for you so you don't get hurt even more."

"Oh, well, I don't want any special treatment. I mean, I can't be the only one who has a blister or two from that hike."

Nelson's eyes glittered with mischief and Hazel found herself totally spellbound. "Maybe not the only one with blisters, but the boss's girlfriend definitely gets special privileges, don't you think?"

Hazel felt a warm blush climbing her neck and into her cheeks. "Except when it's not real," she whispered.

Nelson's playful grin fell, and he cleared his throat. "Yeah. I suppose. But no one else knows that, so…" His eyes darted around the tent. "A neat freak, huh?" He pushed a small smile on his face. "I should have guessed."

Hazel frowned. "What's that supposed to mean?"

Nelson shrugged and rose to his feet just outside the tent door. "It just fits, I guess."

Hazel crossed her arms over her chest and pouted. "Nothing wrong with liking things in their place."

Nelson laughed. "Nothing wrong at all." He held out his hand. "Come on. Dinner's ready."

Hazel answered his smile with one of her own and rose to her feet. Grabbing a pair of flip-flops out of her duffle, she hobbled out of the tent. "Whew!" She stretched her arms. "The air in there gets stuffy."

"Yeah, hazard of the job, I guess." Nelson ran his hand through his dark hair. It reached the bottom of his ears, indicating he hadn't had it cut in a while.

With glorious hair like that, I hope he continues to let it grow. There is something so sexy about a guy's hair being just a little too long.

Nelson started toward the fire and Hazel went to follow him. "Ouch," she muttered quietly as she limped along. "Oh!" She gasped as strong arms suddenly swung her off her feet.

Her arms wrapped around Nelson's neck and she clung tight. "What are you doing?" she demanded even as her girlie side sighed at the show of chivalry.

"Getting to dinner. I'm starving and you're slow." Nelson winked at her and Hazel pinched her lips to keep from smiling.

Rogue. That's the perfect word for this guy. He's a rogue and a flirt and it's no wonder girls in historical novels fall all over themselves.

"You could have just gone on without me, you know," she said, feeling like she needed to fill the silence.

"Now, where's the fun in that? This way, I get to hold a beautiful girl in my arms and get to dinner faster. Much better."

"You, Sir, are incorrigible," Hazel said with a smile.

Nelson set her down next to a log they were using as a bench near the fire pit. "Just what every man wants to hear." He glanced at the group of people watching them. "Why don't you have a seat and I'll bring you over a plate when I'm done helping the crew."

"I can-"

Nelson put a finger to her lips and Hazel nearly closed her eyes to enjoy the sensation. *Oh, Honey, you've got it bad.*

"It won't take long. Take it easy and I'll get to you as soon as I can." He raised his eyebrows.

"Okay," she said in a breathy voice. *Well, if that didn't clue him in to your feelings, I don't know what will.*

Nelson gave her the type of smile that made her sigh and walked toward the waiting crowd. "Who's ready for roasted porcupine?" he yelled in a teasing voice.

"Ewwww!" Mallory said loudly, while Annette giggled. The rest of the group chuckled good naturedly before forming a line at the food table.

Hazel shook her head at Nelson's antics. *He has them eating out of the palm of his hand.* She pursed her lips and huffed a laugh. *Including me.*

"You coming?"

Hazel squeaked and turned at the voice. "Oh, Jack." She put her hand to her heart. "You scared me."

Jack raised an eyebrow and smirked. "What's the matter, not used to having a man so close?" He laughed and sat down so their shoulders touched.

A zing went through Hazel, but not the kind she looked forward to with Nelson's touch. "Uh..." She tried to scoot away without attracting too much attention, but Jack just chuckled and followed her. "Look, Jack, I'm not... you're a nice guy, but... I mean, it's not you-"

Jack tilted his head to the side and folded his arms. "It's just what? I don't have the right bank account? I don't own a resort?"

Hazel's eyes widened in alarm and she jerked to look at Nelson. She found his dark eyes boring a hole into Jack, an easy to read threat in the glare. Unfortunately, he was stuck behind the table helping dish people up, and couldn't do anything about Jack's accusations at the moment.

"That has absolutely nothing to do with anything," Hazel said as she tore her eyes from Nelson and looked back at Jack.

He scoffed. "You haven't even been willing to give me the time of day." He smiled. "If you'd just be willing to spend a little time with me, I think you'd find it worth your while." Jack reached out and grabbed Hazel's hand.

She tried to pull it out of his grip, but he held on tightly.

"Come on, Hazel. Just take a walk with me and you'll see."

"No, thank you," she said as she continued to pull back. "I have a bunch of blisters from the hike and it hurts to walk. I think I'll sit right here and wait for Nelson."

Jack scowled and stood, pulling Hazel with him. "You'll be fine. A couple of blisters are nothing. Come on." He turned and began pulling her toward the far side of the campground.

"Jack!" Hazel hissed, trying not to make a scene. When he didn't stop, she dug in her aching heels, but Jack was too big for her to stop. She ended up stumbling after him, stepping on rocks and twigs in her flimsy shoes. "Jack, I mean it. Stop."

"Just give me a chance," he said over his shoulder.

"I believe she said to stop." Nelson's deep voice sounded angry, but Hazel felt only relief at his interference. She didn't think Jack would actually hurt her, but she also had no intention of being with him long enough to find out.

Jack spun. "What's it to you?" he asked angrily.

"Other than the fact that that's my girlfriend you're dragging along, I have a problem with guys who treat women like they can't think for themselves." Nelson's fists were clenching and unclenching as he stepped closer to Jack and Hazel. "Hazel has repeatedly told you no and you won't listen. She doesn't owe you anything. She doesn't have to hear you out or give you a chance. If she isn't comfortable enough with you to spend time with you, you need to back off and respect that deci-sion," he growled. His chest was heaving and his breath coming out in large huffs. He looked larger than life and ready to pound something into the ground.

Hazel's eyes were wide. A mix of adoration and anxiety rocketed through her. *I've never seen him so angry, but oh my gosh, if that wasn't a swoon worthy speech, I don't know what is. He is the PERFECT hero.*

Jack dropped Hazel's wrist and stepped back a little, putting his hands up. "Look, all I wanted was a chance to get to know her without you and your millions hanging over us."

Hazel snapped her head in Jack's direction. "Jack," she croaked, then cleared her throat. "Jack, my interest in Nelson has nothing to do with his money. I'm sorry-" Nelson growled at her apology, and Hazel winced, but kept going. "I'm sorry if I haven't been as clear as I should. But I'm not interested, plus I'm already with someone else." She almost apologized again, but Nelson had come up behind her and his body ex-uded a protectiveness that helped her hold the words inside. *Nelson's right. I don't owe Jack anything. Even if it feels mean to lay it all out there.*

Nelson's warm hands ran up her arms and gently pushed her to the side and behind his strong body. Hazel fisted the back of his shirt, wor-ried he might leap forward and plant a facer on Jack, who was glaring like he could melt the two of them into a little puddle. *Oh my gosh, he smells good.* She nearly leaned into his back to take a deep whiff, but caught herself just in time. *We're in the middle of an almost-fight and you're smelling your fake boyfriend. What is wrong with you?*

"Let's just get back to the group, huh?" Nelson tilted his head to-ward the fire. "Hazel has made her feelings clear."

Jack spit at Nelson's feet. "Whatever." He started strutting back. "If you ever get tired of slumming with the richies, look me up," Jack sneered over his shoulder.

Nelson turned his body to follow Jack's progress, so Hazel ended up stepping around as well, so she was still at Nelson's back. The further away Jack got, the more the tension in the air dissipated. With a groan, Hazel laid her forehead between Nelson's shoulder blades. "That was terrible."

Nelson turned, dislodging her and gripped her shoulders. It was difficult to see his dark eyes in the dwindling twilight, but from the down-turned shape of his brows, he appeared concerned and Hazel felt another sigh coming on.

"Are you okay?" Nelson asked, his eyes roaming over her.

"Y-yeah. He didn't really hurt me. Just scared me mostly. I don't think he-"

"Do. Not. Excuse him," Nelson ground out. "He is a full grown man and he should know better. You haven't done anything wrong, and he needs to back off. Don't rationalize his behavior."

Hazel blinked and swallowed. "Okay," she squeaked out.

Nelson's face softened again, and he took one hand off her and ran it down his face. "I'm sorry. I shouldn't have gotten so mad, but when I saw him dragging you and-" He cut off mid-sentence and stared at her for several long moments, then with a frustrated growl, he pulled Hazel in and captured her lips with his.

I CAN'T BELIEVE SHE didn't slap me. The thought that he was no better than Jack made Nelson pull back and check Hazel's reaction to his crazy impulse. Her eyes were closed and her hands had started to creep up his chest. As he watched, her eyelids fluttered open.

"Oh!" she said softly. "Is that it?" She jerked after the words left her mouth and even in the semi-dark, Nelson could see a dark red streaming across her cheeks. "I mean- I'm sorry- I shouldn't have-"

Nelson's chuckle was deeper than normal and he pulled her in until his arms were wrapped all the way around her body. "Not even close," he whispered before kissing her again and cutting off her embarrassed rambling.

Excitement mixed with contentment shot through Nelson. He hadn't realized just how much he had wanted to do this very thing. The cute, little sigh that escaped her only made him want more. Hazel must have been feeling the same way, because her hands wrapped around his neck and she rose up on tiptoe to better reach him.

So perfect. How can a woman feel like she is made just for you?

"Boss!" Daniel choked out the word through a cough.

The noise brought Nelson's wandering thoughts to a halt, and he pulled his head back. Hazel's wide, blue eyes opened and looked just as stunned as he felt. *Fake. This is fake, and it's going to be over at the end of the week.* Those words were like a bucket of cold water. Clearing his throat, he let go of her and stepped back.

The disappointment that skittered across her adorable face nearly made him reach out again, but Nelson stuffed his hands in his pockets. "Uh, yeah?" He turned to where Daniel stood smirking behind him. "Whatcha need?"

"Thought you and the little lady might like to eat before dinner gets cold," Daniel raised a knowing eyebrow.

"Oh, yeah. Dinner." Nelson rubbed the back of his overly warm neck. "Come on, Haze. Let's grab something to eat." Without thinking about it, Nelson put out his hand and Hazel latched onto it. Holding her small hand felt like the most natural thing in the world and Nelson didn't even register he was doing so until they walked past the fire and Mallory and Annette pumped their eyebrows and giggled.

Crud. No wait. That's good, right? Everyone is supposed to think we're together... He huffed and ran his free hand through his hair. *Except I'm not supposed to actually get emotionally involved.* He glanced over his shoulder at Hazel. Her eyes were downcast and she let go of his hand to grab a paper plate.

Uh, oh. Now what? Shoot. She's probably worried I'm going to take this too far, when I promised her it would just be for show. Nelson pasted a smile on his face and elbowed Hazel in the arm to get her attention. "We did pretty good back there," he whispered close to her ear.

"What?" Hazel's eyebrows scrunched together.

"You, uh, you followed my lead just right. I think we really sold them on this relationship. Hopefully, that means Jerk-uh, Jack will leave you alone now." Nelson raised his eyebrows expectantly.

Hazel's face fell for only a moment before she smiled back at him. "Oh, yeah. Right. I'll bet it worked like a charm. Thanks so much for being willing to help me out. I'm sure it isn't easy for you." She delicately cleared her throat and looked back at the food they were dishing up.

"Nah," Nelson shoulder bumped her. "No hardship in taking care of a pretty girl."

Hazel dropped her plate, startling him. "Sorry," she murmured, not looking up. "I, uh, I'm starting to get a headache. I think I'll lie down instead of eat." She paused and Nelson could have sworn she sniffed, but the sound was too quiet to be sure. "I'll see you in the morning. Thanks again for your help."

"Sure thing," Nelson turned to watch her scurry back to her tent. Hazel smiled wide and waved at Mallory and Annette, but ignored their invitation to sit with them. Hazel pointed to her head and mouthed the word, 'headache'. Once the other girls nodded their understanding, Hazel quickly closed the distance to her tent and disappeared inside.

"That went well. I didn't know the great Nelson Truman had the ability to scare girls off. I thought they flocked to you like bees to honey." Jerome slung his arm around Nelson's shoulders and laughed.

"Shut up," Nelson muttered. "I didn't drive her off. She had a headache. Probably from dealing with that Jack guy. If he touches her again, I'm not going to be held responsible for my actions." Nelson turned back to the table and piled his plate high before stomping to a seat at the fire.

"Sooo…" Mallory's high voice whined in Nelson's ear like a pesky insect, but he hid the annoyance behind a grin.

"So?" He raised his brows.

"Just how long have you and Hazel been an item?" Mallory plopped down beside him with Annette following.

"Oh. Not long. We're still fairly new to the whole relationship thing." Nelson put his focus on his plate. Pretending through his actions that Hazel and he were dating was one thing, to sit here and verbalize the lie was harder for him. But all he had to do was think about Jack dragging Hazel away from the group and Nelson's protective instincts reared their head.

"Well, I think it's darling that she was willing to come camping with you." Annette giggled as she leaned around Mallory. "She said it was her first time, but she didn't tell us she did it because of you."

Nelson nodded, but kept his mouth too full to answer.

"It's awfully sweet," Mallory sighed. "But I have to admit it put a kink in mine and Annette's plans." She looked coyly at Nelson. "We each had high hopes of our own for getting to know you, but it's easy to see that Hazel is the only one who holds your attention." She pursed her lips and put her shoulders and hands in the air. "Maybe I can get a guy to look at me like that, someday."

"Oooh, me too. It's so adorable how they look all googly-eyed at each other," Annette squealed.

Nelson nearly dropped his plate. "What? Googly-eyed? You're kidding right?" The food he had been eating felt like it was stuck in his throat and he grabbed his water bottle, chugging half of it to clear the blockage.

"Of course not, Silly," Annette waved a hand at him. "Your guy's feelings are written all over your faces." She sighed dreamily. "It's perfect."

Nelson coughed a couple of times and pounded his chest. "Yeah. Perfect." *I guess I'm just a better actor than I thought. Cause that's all it is. Acting. At the end of the week, this is all over. Jack will be gone and so will the danger. Nothing here is real.*

"Hey ladies," Tyler said smoothly as he walked over with Jack tagging along behind him. "They just pulled out stuff for s'mores." He grinned and held out a hand to Mallory. "Come on, I'll help you roast a mallow."

"Sounds good," Mallory said with a wink. Taking the outstretched hand, she rose up and walked with Annette and the men over to the table, gathering their supplies.

I'm running a freakin' dating service. Nelson made a face and shook his head. *Maybe this camping trip wasn't such a bright idea after all.*

CHAPTER 9

Hazel woke up the next morning to those dang birds again, but also with a firm resolve in mind. *You will stop acting like a teenager with a crush and remember that all of this with Nelson is fake. He's helping keep Jack off your back. That's it. That's why he's holding your hand, it's why he keeps track of you, and it's definitely why he kissed you.*

Her mental pep talk didn't seem to ease the ache in her heart, but she knew there was little that would get rid of that except for time. "At least you're getting good material for a new book," she muttered as she burrowed deeper into the sleeping bag.

While she had been crying into her pillow last night, an idea for a new story had finally popped into her head. Forcing down her tears, she had pulled out her handy notebook and started writing down everything that had happened over the past few days. If she added a bit of exaggeration to the characters, who could blame her?

Jack's overconfident attitude might have become just a little more slimy. While Nelson's heroic acts practically made him angelic. As for the heroine? Hazel decided the girl who got Nelson's attention would be the complete opposite of herself. *He deserves someone outgoing and fun, not shy and scared.*

Hazel risked the cool morning air and reached across the small tent for her notebook again. She began scribbling furiously as new ideas ran through her mind. "My readers are going to love this. I mean, who wouldn't love a hunky, billionaire hero?"

"You going to get up? Or do I need to get the bullhorn?" Nelson's teasing voice came from outside her tent.

Hazel jerked and dropped her pencil. Glancing at her watch, she realized it was later than she thought. "Oh! Sorry! I'm coming! No need for the bullhorn." She put her stuff away and began to climb out of bed. "Although, it might actually scare away all those noisy birds, so... there's that."

"Okay..." Nelson chuckled. "See you in a few."

Hazel shivered a little as she got dressed. "Why does it have to be so cold in the morning?" After pulling on her shirt, she paused and sniffed. "Oh no." Leaning her head into her armpit, she took a slight whiff. "Oh man... One should never go three days without a shower." Making a disgusted face, she grabbed her deodorant and plied it on thickly. "I wonder if a swim in the pond would help?" She pursed her lips. "It certainly can't hurt. Sheesh. Next time I'm only camping with other stinky girls. Not handsome men."

After spraying her hair with dry shampoo, she emerged from the tent to discover she was the last one awake.

"Morning, Sleeping Beauty," Jack called from his seat at the fire. He grinned before stuffing french toast into his mouth.

Hazel's stomach growled even as she felt a little sick at his term of endearment. *When is he going to leave me alone?* "Uh... morning," she muttered, then hurried to the end of the breakfast line.

Grabbing a plate, Hazel's eyes widened at the display. "Wow. How in the world did we get all this for breakfast up here?" Fresh fruit salad sat next to sausage links and bacon and a large container of french toast sent the heavenly smell of vanilla and cinnamon into the air.

"Hayden sent it up first thing this morning." Nelson said as he stepped up to her side. "Did you sleep okay? Is your headache better?"

Hazel turned to look into his dark brown eyes and found her tongue stuck to the roof of her mouth. *I am such an idiot. Remember the talk this morning! Fake! He's a book hero, not for real life!* "Mmm-myeah..." she managed to get out. "Yeah, just fine until those kamikaze birds went at it again."

Nelson threw his head back and laughed. The sound was rich and full in the early morning air.

I have got to remember to put that in my book. Forcing herself into action, Hazel filled her plate and stuffed a bite of bacon in her mouth, so she couldn't say anything else stupid.

"Go ahead and eat and I'll talk to you later, 'kay?" Nelson leaned in and pecked her temple, before striding over to where his workers were putting stuff together for today's activities.

Hazel had frozen at his touch and it took every ounce of willpower she had not to close her eyes and savor the sensation of his kiss. *Someday I'm going to find a magic pen that lets me bring to life whatever I write. Then I'm going to write a happy ever after for myself. And it's going to be with Nelson Truman.*

With a weary sigh, Hazel put her body back into action. "Sometimes real life stinks," she grumbled as she turned to go sit down and eat.

"Come sit with us, Chica!" Mallory waved her arm frantically at Hazel.

Hazel smiled as she chewed and walked over to the two exuberant women.

"Have a seat," Annette said with a wink, as she scooted over on the log. "So..." Annette had a coy look on her face. "Tell us all about your hunky man over there."

Hazel's eyes bugged out, and she choked on her mouthful of bacon.

"Whoa!" Mallory started pounding her on the back, but Hazel just kept coughing.

Tears were streaming down Hazel's cheeks as she tried to suck in air through her blocked passageways. "Water!" she rasped out, trying to lean away from Mallory's vicious slapping.

Her head bent down as she continued to cough and a bottle of cold water was shoved into her hand. Hazel quickly unscrewed the lid and chugged down half of it, washing down the food.

Bringing the bottle down, she sucked in a large gulp of air. "Ahhh…" she sighed. Closing her eyes, she let herself breathe for a moment, feeling the heat recede from her face and the tears dry on her cheeks.

"Looks like I just saved you," a male voice said up against her ear.

"AHH!" Hazel screamed and jumped up from her place, dumping her plate of food on the ground. *Oh man! And that french toast smelled so good! Are you kidding me?* New tears pricked her eyes, and she looked at the ruined food and listened to the snickering around her.

"Jack!" Mallory jumped to her feet and put her hands on her hips. "That wasn't cool at all! Leave the poor girl alone!"

Jack chuckled and folded his arms over his chest. "I don't know. It was pretty awesome. And now I'm thinking that she owes me for saving her life."

Hazel's whole body was flaming from the embarrassment and attention she was getting this morning. *What is this guy's problem? Why can't he just leave me be?* But despite her anger, Hazel hated that she would never have the courage to say anything. Confrontation scared her more than heights… or getting eaten by a bear. Instead, she clenched her jaw and her fists before bending to the ground to pick up the food so she could throw it away.

"She doesn't owe you a thing, you big meanie," Annette chimed in. Both girls dropped next to Hazel. Mallory put her arms around Hazel's shoulders while Annette picked up the rest of the food.

The girls might have been barely out of high school, but at the moment, Hazel was so grateful for their support she could have kissed them.

"Come on, Girlie. We've got ya." Mallory helped Hazel to her feet, but they didn't make it very far before Jack stepped in front of them.

"Ah, come on, Jack." Annette rolled her eyes. "Haven't you done enough?"

Jack grinned mischievously. "Look," he spread his hands out in front of him, "all I want is a little ole kiss for saving her. No biggie at all."

"What?" Hazel screeched.

Mallory and Annette began giggling. "I think you've got your answer, Hero Boy."

Jack frowned. "If richie over there had saved you, you would have given him a kiss."

"That's because he's her boyfriend, you dolt. When are you going to give up?"

Jack scowled. "When I actually believe they're dating. I think it's all some stupid act." He waved an arm at Hazel. "She won't even give me a chance!"

"There's no law that says she has to," Nelson's deep voice broke up the argument.

Hazel closed her eyes. As much as she loved having Nelson around, it seemed that she was always in some kind of trouble. *Could life be any more unfair? I'm aware I'm not the type of girl he'd go for, but does fate have to keep shoving that in my face?*

"Come on, Haze." Nelson kept his glare on Jack, but held out his hand for Hazel. "We'll get you something else to eat."

Hazel slipped her clammy fingers into his warm ones. As she walked away with Nelson, she could hear Annette and Mallory arguing back and forth with Jack and she shook her head.

"What are you thinking?" Nelson whispered in her ear.

Funny. Him being so close to my ear doesn't freak me out at all. She cleared her throat. "Oh, just thinking I should have stuck to my introvert lifestyle and stayed home. I'm becoming nothing but a burden." *Wow. Way to sound like a whiny, little girl, Hazel. Just what every man wants.*

Nelson shook his head and scoffed. "Sweetheart, it wouldn't have mattered. You're way too cute for men to leave you alone."

Hazel's face jerked toward his. "W-what?"

Nelson grinned and tucked a piece of hair behind her ear. "Don't tell me you've never heard that before? There's a reason Jack isn't giving up, and it's not because of me. He's just as attracted to you as I am."

Hazel blinked, but didn't speak, meanwhile her brain was running at a hundred miles per hour. *He thinks I'm cute. He's attracted to me. Maybe fate isn't so horrible after all.*

Nelson laughed and took the plate from her hands, throwing it in the garbage. "You're acting like no one has ever given you a compliment before." He chuckled a little more. "Come on, let's grab you some food. We don't want you fainting on the hike today."

His teasing finally snapped Hazel out of her stupor and she snorted a laugh. "Eh, I might be out of shape, but I'm way too hearty to faint."

Nelson put his arm around her shoulders and pulled her in until his mouth was right on her ear. "You're perfect, Hazel. Never think otherwise."

NELSON COULD HAVE SMACKED himself this morning. Although he meant every word he was saying to Hazel, he knew it wasn't nice to play with her feelings. *I can't keep her past this week, so why am I saying things like this? I'm going to give her the wrong impression.*

When she had been choking, Nelson had almost leapt over the table to go help her, but Mallory and Annette were there and then Jack handed her the water, so he stayed back, grateful when he saw her take a good breath.

But when Jack had scared her so bad that she had dropped her food, Nelson about lost it. He'd been helping his team pack the rain ponchos for their hike today, and he had almost dropped them in the dirt in order to go help her. Scrambling to catch the supplies, Nelson had hurried through packing them and then darted over to the group. Not for the first time, Nelson had been grateful for the young women who were standing up for Hazel.

Hazel's cheeks had been fiery red and her eyes watery. *I'm seriously going to punch that guy's lights out if he doesn't leave her alone.* Then Jack had demanded a kiss, and it took all of Nelson's willpower not to throw the punch right then and there. *I was angry because no one should be treated like that, not because I was jealous. Definitely not jealous. Nope. Not even a little bit.*

Luckily, Hazel's shock at the request had stalled Jack's progress. Nelson chuckled as he recalled the annoyed look on Jack's face when he had shown up and Hazel had willingly gone with him.

Nelson glanced down at the plate in Hazel's hands, there was hardly anything on it. "Need help? You don't seem to be getting very much."

"I don't think I'm super hungry," Hazel whispered. "But thank you for standing up for me back there. I don't know why he won't just take a hint. I've tried telling him several times I'm not interested."

Nelson tamped down the concern he felt at Hazel not eating much. *She's an adult, you idiot. If she doesn't want to eat, she doesn't have to.* This quiet, inexperienced woman had him acting like a caveman, bringing out every protective instinct he had and Nelson wasn't sure what to do about it. "Yeah, well... at this point it's more about saving face. You've become a challenge, and he doesn't want to lose." Nelson shrugged and decided to move onto another topic before he went back and gave Jack the smack down he deserved.

"You ready for today?" Nelson asked, snatching a piece of orange from her plate.

Hazel grinned and her eyes, previously sad, now twinkled with excitement. "Absolutely. What's on the agenda?"

Nelson swallowed hard. *Geez, all she has to do is smile and I'm tied in knots.* "Uh, today we're hiking up to one of the best viewpoints in the area." Nelson tugged on the collar of his t-shirt, suddenly feeling overly warm in the cool morning air.

"Ooh. I'll have to be sure to bring my camera." Hazel scrunched her lips to one side. "I'm pretty sure my phone is dead by now, so no pictures on that thing."

Nelson chuckled. "Yeah. I heard Luke complaining to his parents this morning that his battery was dead." Nelson dropped his voice to a whisper. "I'm not sure what he thought he could do on it anyway. He hasn't had a signal since we got here."

Hazel shrugged and giggled. "Maybe he just wanted to play games. Most kids don't look up from their phones at all. I was surprised how much he enjoyed the swimming hole the other day."

Nelson nodded. "Yeah. That was pretty awesome." He glanced around before whispering again. "And I have to admit that I thought those two girls who keep coming to your rescue would be all over their phones too. They've surprised me quite a bit on this trip."

Hazel's eyes dimmed just a touch before she rallied. "Yeah. They've been great. Although, they keep trying to get me alone to ask about you, but Jack always interrupts."

Nelson set her plate to the side and wrapped his arms around her waist, pulling her in. "And just what would you tell them if he didn't interrupt? Hmm? Would you tell them how you have the best boyfriend in the world? How I'm so awesome, I bring you on hikes that blister your feet and make you jump off of waterfalls that scare the pajeebies out of you?" Nelson leaned in and nuzzled her neck, loving the fresh smell of Hazel's skin. *No perfume, just fresh, and clean. Perfect.*

Hazel laughed and pushed on his chest. "First of all, that tickles."

Nelson's eyes widened, and he grinned and bent down, fully ready to go at it again.

But Hazel pushed his chest a little harder to stop him. "Second of all, I think I would."

Nelson frowned. "You think you would what?" *What were we talking about?*

"I would tell them I had the best boyfriend in the world. One who was patient with my bumbling behaviors. One who doesn't seem to be embarrassed every time I trip or do something stupid. One who says sweet things in my ear. One who comes to my rescue every time I'm backed into a corner." Her eyes softened and a small smile graced her lovely, pink lips. "And one who has set his own needs and desires aside to make sure I'm safe, even if he doesn't want to."

Nelson was frozen. *She can't be describing me? No one ever talks about me like I'm some kind of hero.*

Hazel's cheeks blushed a deep red and Nelson couldn't help but touch the heated skin.

"Sorry." She cleared her throat and looked to the side. "That was probably a bit much for a fake relationship."

Nelson forced a chuckle. "I guess it just goes to show that you must be an awesome author. You've definitely got a way with words."

Hazel smiled, but it didn't reach her eyes. "I'd better go get ready. I don't want to hold up the group."

Nelson nodded and stepped back from her. "Oh!" He slapped his forehead. "Hang on a sec. I got something for you." He jogged over his own tent and grabbed a small package out of his supplies. Coming back, he held it out to Hazel. "Here."

Hazel took it and turned it over. "Thanks. What is it?"

A real smile graced Nelson's face. "It's moleskin."

Hazel looked up at him skeptically. "Mole skin? Like from a real mole?"

Nelson laughed and shook his head. "That'd be cool, but nah. This is something you put on blisters so you don't get hurt anymore. Look." Nelson turned the package over and showed her the directions on the back. "Just follow the instructions and you won't make your feet any worse today. I'd hate for you to not be able to walk tomorrow."

"Yeah, having you carry me everywhere would be absolute torture," Hazel said as she rolled her eyes.

Nelson barked out a disbelieving laugh. "Every time I decide you're just a quiet, meek thing, you burst out with something flirtatious." He grinned. "Always keeping me on my toes."

"Sorry, I shouldn't have said that." Hazel wrinkled her freckled nose. "But thank you. I'm not sure anyone has ever watched out for me as much as you do."

If he didn't know better, Nelson would have sworn that her blue gaze was full of genuine adoration. *That's ridiculous. I'm no one's hero. I'm the irresponsible floater.*

"Anyway, thanks. I'll go get this on." She ducked her head and walked back to her tent.

Nelson watched her go and sighed. *Fake. Fake. Fake. Remember, you dork, it's all fake.* Unfortunately, the feelings he was fighting felt all too real.

CHAPTER 10

Hazel snapped what seemed like her hundredth picture. "Oh my word, it's gorgeous up here!" she mumbled to herself as she looked at the small digital screen in front of her. "This stupid camera doesn't do it justice."

"Seriously," Mallory said from Hazel's right side, holding up her own camera. Only hers had a long lens on it and Mallory was down on one knee, angling the camera every which way, then manually adjusting things.

"Whoa," Hazel said softly. "You must really like photography."

Mallory grinned up at her. "Yeah. I actually prefer things like weddings, but I love to take pictures."

Hazel grinned. *I'd have never thought that just looking at her. Note to self. Don't judge a book by its cover.* "You going to do it as a career?"

Mallory stood up and shrugged. "I dunno. I mean, I love it, but it can be so hard to break into the business. Especially in weddings." Mallory fiddled with her lens cap. "I need a portfolio to really get started and I don't have one." She glanced up, her eyes sad. "My dad wants me to go to college and get a degree in business, but..." Her eyes went back to the gorgeous forest view. "I just can't see myself sitting through another four years of boring classes, listening to those teachers drone on when I could be snapping photos."

"You could always study photography. That wouldn't be quite as boring," Hazel pointed out.

"I could." Mallory nodded. "But what I really want is field work. I want to get out and get it going." She grinned. "I guess I'm not a super patient person. Maybe if someone would just be willing to let me do their wedding, then I could get a jump start and show my dad that I can do it."

Hazel frowned. "Do you know anyone getting married soon? Would they be willing to hire you?"

Mallory gave Hazel a smirk. "Oh, I don't know. I mean, I don't know anyone who's engaged, but I've met this darling couple."

Hazel raised a suspicious eyebrow. "Oh, really? Anyone I know?" She did her best to keep her voice steady. *She can't mean that Nelson and I are darling, can she? He's so far out of my league it isn't even funny. The only reason we're dating is because he's like some crazy superhero, saving me from Jack.*

Mallory laughed. "Oh, go on. You know I'm talking about you and that cute Nelson. You two are just perfect together. And seriously, that kiss the other night?" Mallory fanned herself. "Whoo! If I'd had my camera on me, I would have captured that one for sure!"

Hazel laughed nervously and fiddled with her camera. "You're sweet, but it isn't like that."

"Isn't like what?" Mallory asked as she went back to snapping photos.

"Oh, nothing." Hazel walked away from the edge of the mountain and plopped down on the ground with a groan. She took a good look at her ankles to see if she had gotten any more blisters during the day. "So far, so good."

"Feet okay?" Nelson asked as he sat down next to her.

"Yeah, surprisingly. Thanks so much for sharing your skin stuff."

Nelson laughed. "Moleskin."

Hazel joined in his mirth. "Yeah, that. Sheesh. I had no idea that camping was so tiring." She put her hand over her mouth as she yawned. "I think I might sleep for a week when we get back."

Nelson put one knee up and rested an arm on it. "Yeah. I'm usually pretty worn out, but I love it." He faced the forest view and Hazel studied his handsome profile.

Oh yeah... perfect book boyfriend material. The only sad part about going home to write this book will be leaving him behind. She sighed and poked at the ground with a stick. *Not that he'll care. I'm just a quiet girl he has to keep rescuing, but now I've been dumb enough to go and start falling for him. Dumb, dumb, dumb.*

"Why the sigh?" Nelson tilted his head and scrunched his eyebrows. "Aren't you enjoying yourself?"

"Oh, yeah. Sorry." Hazel scrunched her nose. "I'm loving it, I was just thinking about the book I'm going to write when I get home."

Nelson's eyebrows shot up and interest lit his gaze. "Oh, yeah? What's it going to be about? Besides all that gushy romance stuff." He waved his hand in the air.

Hazel laughed. "Gushy romance stuff? I'll have you know that romance is one of the biggest genres in the book world, Buddy!"

"Yeah, but it's also dominated by women. I, if you haven't noticed, am a man." He pumped his eyebrows. "I don't want to hear about the lovey stuff, just the rest of the action."

Hazel shoulder bumped him. "Well, the story revolves around the lovey stuff, so... there's not a whole lot left. But, I told you before, I came camping to broaden my horizons, so I could write more realistic stuff." She pursed her lips and tilted her head back and forth, her eyes focused on the horizon. "So, maybe I'll write a story about a girl who goes camping."

"Hmmm..." Nelson put his chin between two fingers and nodded sagely. "Sounds good. And what exactly happens on this camping trip?"

"Well, the girl has to meet a cute guy, obviously."

Nelson made his eyebrows dance again. "Yeah, we can't forget that. But what else?"

Hazel wasn't ready to tell him she wanted to write their story, so she came up with another idea. "Maybe she somehow gets separated from the group?"

"Yeah!" Nelson's eyes lit up, and he leaned toward her eagerly. "And then she runs into a bear."

Hazel grimaced. "Please tell me I don't have to have personal experience with that one to write about it."

Nelson threw an arm around her shoulders. "Nah. But don't worry, I've got bear spray if we need it."

"Then let's pray we don't need it."

Nelson chuckled. "Okay. She runs into a bear. Then what?"

"The cute guy has to come save her, of course!" Hazel threw up her hands with a smile.

"Why can't she save herself?" Nelson frowned.

"Because it's a romance. And having the guy save her makes it more *ro-man-tic*." Hazel slowed down the last word and emphasized each syllable.

Nelson grinned. "Not for the guys. Watching a girl win against a bear would definitely be romantic for a guy."

"Good thing most of my audience is women then," Hazel said with a grin. *And I guess that puts an end to the question of whether Nelson could ever be attracted to me or not. I'm not bear-fighting material.*

"Yep. Good thing." Nelson tucked a stray piece of hair behind her ear and Hazel fought not to show the shiver that went through her at his tender touch.

ONLY TWO MORE DAYS. Two more days. Nelson couldn't seem to stop talking to or touching Hazel. Here they'd been in the mountains for days without a shower or bathroom and she seemed as fresh as a daisy. *How do girls do it?*

"So I take it you've never read a romance?" Hazel asked with her eyebrows raised expectantly.

"Uh, no," Nelson answered with a shake of his head. "I've been known to get a little crazy sometimes, but never that crazy."

"What?" Hazel gasped. "It's not crazy to read a romance! Thousands of people do it every day!"

"You mean thousands of women do every day. Us men have better things to do." Nelson breathed on his fingernails and rubbed them on his chest.

"Men read them too!" Hazel bit her lip for a second, holding back a grin. "Those are probably the men who have girlfriends. You know, because they understand what women want from reading those books."

Oh, she did not just go there. "My dear, Hazel. That distinctly sounds like a challenge."

Hazel's eyes widened. "Uh, no, I wasn't-"

Nelson couldn't help it. She flustered so easily and was so cute when it happened. Putting on his best 'smolder' he leaned in, making sure to keep eye contact. "Are you accusing me of not knowing what women want? That's mighty low of you. Girlfriends are supposed to be supportive of their men." Nelson kept going, leaning in until they were nose to nose. "Maybe those men read those books because they *don't* know what women want, while the rest of us are just naturals at it." He quirked an eyebrow and let one side of his mouth lift in a grin he knew girls loved.

Hazel looked liked a deer caught in the headlights. Her eyes were wide and her cheeks were pink. Her mouth kept opening slightly and closing, as if she wanted to speak but couldn't figure out what to say. Nelson stayed in close, allowing them to share the same air, but when Hazel never recovered enough to speak, he leaned back, pushing aside the fact that she hadn't been pulled in. *So much for my woman skills. No wonder my brothers always get the attention.*

However, when his face had moved back a bit, her eyes darted to his lips and back up, causing Nelson to pause. *Yes!* He mentally threw a fist in the air. *Maybe she is attracted and she's just too shy to do anything about it.* "Well, I'm not," he murmured out loud, leaning in and pressing his lips to hers.

The kiss was light, but lingering. Nelson had convinced himself that the sparks from their first kiss a couple of days ago had been imagined. *No one can be perfect for someone else, can they?* But feeling her soft mouth and hearing her almost imperceptible sigh, sent a jolt through him that let him know it was much more than his imagination.

He pulled back and chuckled when she followed him. The sound of his laugh, caused Hazel's eyes to shoot open. She blinked rapidly for a moment as if getting her bearings. "Oh...." she whispered.

Yeah. Oh. Dang, I shouldn't have done that. I'm starting to get in way too deep here. Nelson cleared his throat and leaned all the way upright. "See? I told you I know what women want." He cringed even as he said the words. He knew immediately that his attempt to distance himself was going to hurt Hazel.

Hazel flinched at his comment, but quickly recovered. Pasting a pleasant smile on her face, she turned away from him. "Yep. I guess you don't need to read those romance novels after all." She took a deep breath. "If you'll excuse me." Standing up, she brushed off her backside and walked back toward Mallory and Annette.

Nelson's shoulders fell, and he hung his head. *Way to go, Jerk.* He scrubbed his face with his hands. "But seriously, what else was I supposed to do?" he grumbled to himself. "This is fake, and in two days she's leaving. It would never work, even if I was looking for something long term." He watched Hazel smile and nod at whatever story Annette was telling as if her world hadn't just been upended with that kiss like Nelson's had. *And Hazel isn't the type of girl to have a fling with. She's a white picket fence, a baby on each hip kind of girl. And I'm not ready to give that to anyone... even her.*

Groaning, Nelson forced thoughts of Hazel and babies out of his head and stood. "Everybody ready to go back?" Nelson cupped his hand around his mouth as he shouted.

A general groaning could be heard as people started to pick themselves up off the ground.

Nelson laughed. "We can sleep here, that's fi-"

His voice was cut off with a sudden crack of thunder.

"Whoa." Nelson jerked his head toward the rumbling along with the rest of the group. *Well, there's the storm my app said was coming.* Not far in the distance was a dark group of clouds and even as they stared at the impending weather, a flash of lightning shot across the system. "Okey doke, people! Let's get a move on. We'll be much happier if we can get back to the campsite before that storm hits us."

Nelson quickly walked around to make sure everyone had their gear, particularly their cameras, stored safely.

"Are we going to be alright?" Luke's mother asked as she grabbed Nelson's arm in a death grip. Worry emanated from her and her eyes kept darting back to the dark clouds quickly coming toward them.

"Yeah. No worries," Nelson said soothingly. "We're going to be alright. We might get wet, but once we're back, bundled into our tents, it'll be fine."

She nodded nervously and went back to making sure her children's backpacks were on.

Time to get a move on, Nelson thought to himself. *That storm is gonna be a doozy.* "Haze!" Nelson searched until he found her and reached out his hand. Hazel's eyes widened for a moment before she came forward to put her hand into his. "Let's move!" Nelson took off at a rapid clip, hoping to outrun the storm, but knowing their odds weren't good. He chose to keep his focus on that rather than the fact that he had needed Hazel at his side. Knowing she was near and safe helped keep him grounded. *It's just because you feel protective of her. She's easily taken advantage of and it's your job to prevent that. That's all it is. Nothing more. Now worry about that storm. It's more important.*

CHAPTER 11

Hazel moved her legs quickly to keep up with Nelson, who was practically running in his attempt to get back before the storm hit. Every time she heard the thunder rumbling behind her, the quake seemed to go through her very bones. "It's okay, we're safe. We're going to be fine," she whispered to herself.

Ever since she was a kid, Hazel had hated thunder and lightning storms. It had stemmed from an incident where lightning had struck the ground only a hundred feet from her house. The entire house had shook and Hazel had thought the windows were going to shatter. The air had been electric for several moments after it had happened.

She shivered at the memory. *I never want to go through that again.* With firm determination, she pushed herself to keep up with Nelson's pace, eager to be in her tent and away from the storm.

"You okay?" Nelson asked over his shoulder. "I can hear you talking to yourself."

Ah, crud. Way to make yourself look even more loony. "Yeah, I'm fine," she lied. "I just don't love storms, so I'm ready for us to get back to the campsite.

"Really?" He faced forward again. "I've always loved storms. They're gorgeous. But I'm not a big fan of hiking in the rain. Nothing worse than squishy, wet socks."

Hazel laughed uneasily as another rumble went through the air. "Yeah. I can imagine that wouldn't be fun."

"So, what do you not like?"

Hazel's gaze shifted from looking at the clouds back to Nelson. "What?"

"What do you not like about storms?" he clarified.

"Oh. I, uh, I just don't like them in general, I guess. I'm a bit of a fraidy cat."

Nelson frowned, but didn't say anything else and Hazel was beyond grateful that he let it go. *If a man thinks a woman fighting a bear is romantic, what in the world would he think of one who is scared of thunder and lightning?*

"Well, on the plus side, our hike is downhill, so we can move a little faster than our way up."

"Yeah. That's good. Also good for my thighs. They've been put through more work this week than I think they've been in the last five years." She stumbled on a rock, but quickly righted herself.

"Have you been sore?"

"Oh, yeah. But it's no big deal. I needed to get off my tush and do something. Besides, I plan to eat all the weight I lost back in Oreos, so..." she shrugged, "it's all worth it."

Nelson laughed and continued guiding her down the path. "Well, not that my words mean much, but I don't think you need to get off your tush. You look great."

Hazel felt her telltale blush jump into her cheeks and was grateful that Nelson was watching the trail when he said those words. They had come out so easily and Hazel couldn't tell if that meant that he said things like that all the time, or if it meant they were sincere. *I'm going to pretend it was sincere. After all, isn't that what a book boyfriend would do?* "Thank you," she said softly.

Nelson grinned over his shoulder at her before going back to the path.

Hazel jumped when the thunder let loose once again. *This is going to be a long night.*

NELSON PULLED THE HOOD of his poncho over his face better. "Geez, now I know what they mean when they say it's raining buckets," he grumbled.

"Seriously," Daniel growled. "This is ridiculous."

"At least the food is warm. Thank you, Hayden," Nelson muttered. Hayden had sent up packages of beef stew and rolls the day before and with the wet weather, it seemed like the perfect night to heat it up and warm themselves from the insides out.

Nelson had practically sprinted the last mile to the campsite in order to beat the storm, but his pushing had paid off. Not ten minutes after he had gotten everyone tucked into their tents with specific instructions not to come out unless it was an emergency, the sky had opened up.

Nelson and his crew had grabbed their ponchos and pulled them on, then headed toward the food area. Luckily, they had covered the food tables with a tarp when they had set up camp, so none of the food was wet. But they had had to pull out a propane stove in order to heat everything, since there was no way to start a fire in this downpour.

"Alright. We can use that tray over there and start delivering bowls to tents. Sound good?" Nelson asked.

A chorus of yeses met his ears. *I am so ready to lay down for the night, but duty calls.* He snorted. *And my brothers think I play all day. Maybe they need to try hiking and camping in a rainstorm.*

One by one, the men began delivering the meal to the worn out campers, and soon they were nearly done. "I'll take Hazel's with me," Nelson said as he grabbed two of the last bowls. "You guys go ahead and deliver Jack's and Tyler's and then hunker down for the night, huh?"

Daniel smirked at him. "Got it, Boss. You know, you look pretty tired. I could always deliver Ms. Thurgood's if you wanted to head straight to your tent."

Nelson rolled his eyes. "You guys are hilarious. I got it."

"I'll bet you do," Daniel muttered.

"Buzz off," Nelson growled.

Daniel put his hands up. "Didn't mean anything by it. We've just been enjoying the show this week. Never seen you pay attention to one girl this long before."

"Yeah well, Hazel is…" Nelson searched for the right word. "She's… different. Plus, I'm mostly trying to help keep Jack off her back," he brought his voice down to a whisper for the last sentence.

Daniel's eyebrows shot up. "Really? You don't have any feelings for her at all?"

Nelson paused. *Do I? I enjoy being around her. I'm definitely attracted to her. But I'm not ready to settle. There's no way any of this is real. It's all just heat of the moment stuff.* Nelson shook his head and said the word even though it felt sour on his lips. "Nope."

Daniel leaned back and folded his arms over his chest. "Well, you deserve an award then, because you sure had me fooled."

Nelson shrugged and tried to keep the blush on his neck from creeping into his face. "Yeah, well. It's no biggie. Gotta run."

They watched him but didn't speak as he sprinted through the rain to Hazel's tent door. Standing as far under her rain flap at he could, he called out to her. "Hey, Haze? I've got dinner. You awake?"

"Coming!"

Nelson could hear shuffling and then the sound of the zipper as she opened her door. "Oh my goodness! You're getting drenched! Get in here!" Hazel reached up and grabbed the bowls and bag of rolls from him, then scurried backward so he had room to enter.

Turning his back to the tent, Nelson slipped out of his poncho and stepped out of his boots, before stepping back in the tent and sitting down. After he closed up the door, he sighed. "Dude, a man could drown in that weather."

Hazel nodded, then jumped at a rumble in the distance. "Or, you know, die," she grumbled as she wiggled around and situated herself on her sleeping bag.

Nelson grinned. "I don't think anyone is in danger of dying. It's too wet for a fire to start and the lightning isn't directly overhead. So, no danger of it striking trees near us. We're perfectly safe."

Hazel hummed an uncertain agreement, but didn't argue with him.

Looking closer, Nelson could see that she was trembling, and it immediately put his protective instincts into high gear. "Are you cold? Or still scared?" He got on his knees and scooted closer to her.

"Uh, probably a little of both." Hazel looked down as if just now realizing she still held their food. "Here." She shoved one of the bowls at him. "Better to eat it while it's hot, right?"

"Right." Nelson took the bowl and used it to warm his cold hands.

Together, they said a blessing and then dug into the delicious stew.

"Oh my word, your brother can cook for me any day!" Hazel moaned as she took another large bite.

A surge of jealousy ripped through Nelson and he nearly jerked to his feet in surprise. *Whoa. Where did that come from?* He cleared his throat to get rid of the uncomfortable sensation. "Yeah. He's really good at what he does, even if he does wear a dumb hat and skirt."

Hazel paused with her spoon halfway to her mouth. "Skirt? What do you mean?"

Nelson raised an eyebrow at her. "An apron. He wears an apron. It looks like a skirt."

Hazel pinched her lips between her teeth. "Nelson Truman, are you jealous of your brother?"

Nelson jerked back as if he had been slapped. "What?"

Hazel shrugged while finishing chewing. "You sound like you're jealous of him. Why in the world would someone like you be jealous of anybody?"

Nelson narrowed his eyes and tilted his head. "Someone like me? What does that mean?"

Hazel's eyes dropped to her bowl, and she pushed the food around with her spoon. Nelson could see her blush crawling across her cheeks and it made him want to reach out and touch her soft skin. Instead, he tightened his fingers around his spoon and forced another bite in his mouth.

"Well, you're the kind of guy other people are jealous of. Not the kind that needs to be jealous."

Now it was Nelson's turn to pause with food halfway to his mouth. "Me?" he scoffed. "Are you kidding? I'm the lazy bum of the family. The moocher. Nobody would ever be jealous of me."

Hazel's eyebrows turned down in concern. "Lazy bum? Moocher? Neither of those fits the man I've come to know over the last few days." She set her bowl down and the volume of her voice rose. "For goodness sake, Nelson. You run an entire business! With several employees! You're a billionaire, and yet you work way more hours than the normal person. Plus you have more knowledge about the outdoors than I could ever hope to know. You've dealt with thunderstorms, terrified authors, surly teenagers, and rude, single men. And you've done it all without anger or being rude back! Not to mention," she threw her hands in the air, "you're one of the most handsome men I have ever met in my life. Your hair, well, your hair is just made for a woman to run her fingers through, and crikey, you still smell good and we haven't had showers in days! How do you do it?"

Hazel was breathing heavy as she finished her little tirade and Nelson found his own breaths matching hers. *Does she really mean all that or is she just trying to make me feel better because I've been helping her?* "You must see the world through rose-colored glasses, because I can guarantee you that nobody in my family thinks those things of me." He couldn't help but lean in and tease her. "And I don't think I want any of them talking about how handsome I am. That would just be weird."

Hazel snorted a laugh as she took a bite of roll.

Unable to resist, Nelson reached out and fingered a lock of her hair. "And speaking of hair, yours is amazing. I've noticed it smells like..." he lifted it to his nose and took a deep whiff, "hm... hard to place. Ocean breeze?"

Hazel's eyes were wide. "Umm... close. It's Tropical Breeze. It's my dry shampoo."

Nelson kept his eyes on hers. *Wow, they are so blue. Why does she have to be so irresistible?*

"Truth is, if I use that stuff any more days, my hair will probably stand straight up from being so gunked up."

Nelson tugged on her hair gently, pulling her close. "You'd still be adorable," he murmured, his lips grazing her cheek. He smiled at her intake of breath. Nelson ran his nose along her cheek, loving the red that colored her skin everywhere he could see.

Hazel reach up and ran a trembling hand through his hair.

Closing his eyes, Nelson nearly groaned at the contact. "I haven't used any of that girlie stuff. Being creek washed probably doesn't make it smell as nice."

"You smell like pine and rain," Hazel whispered.

Nelson could take no more. The air in the tent was nearly as electric as the sky outside and he wanted, no... needed, to kiss her. Not for show. Not to scare off Jack, but just because he wanted to. Just because she looked at him like he was a superhero. Just because she was so beautiful, he couldn't help himself.

Leaving her cheek, he came in front of her and placed a light kiss at the edge of her mouth. He could feel her body trembling, and he hoped some of it had to do with him and not the cold, because he felt as if he were on fire. *She has to feel it too, right?*

He kissed the other side of her mouth, then gently rubbed his lips across hers.

"Nelson," she whispered.

"Yes?"

"I really need you to kiss me right now." Her tone was quiet, almost reverent.

Nelson couldn't help but chuckle. "Your wish is my command." Finally, blessedly, he put his mouth to hers fully and took what he had been dreaming of.

DREAMING. I HAVE TO *be dreaming.* As Nelson grabbed the back of her neck and pulled her in tighter, Hazel nearly melted. Her mind frantically catalogued every sensation and movement, knowing if she didn't recreate this in her book, she would forever regret it.

Nelson Truman is what fantasies are made of and I get to experience it first hand.

A loud clap of thunder shook Hazel from her pleasure-induced stupor. She jumped back and gasped. Her trembling fingers rose to her lips, and she stared at Nelson, who stared back with unabashed interest. "Th-thank you," she stuttered.

Nelson blinked, then frowned. "For what?"

"For indulging my girlie fantasies. You've been so great with helping me steer clear of Jack this week, which I'm sure hasn't been easy for you, and now, to be willing to kiss me because I asked you to... well, I'll never forget it."

Hazel could have slapped herself. It was becoming more and more clear to her that her brain failed to function properly whenever she was around the handsome man.

Nelson's eyebrows shot up and he leaned back. "Oh. Yeah. Well, you know..." He rubbed the back of his neck and laughed uncomfortably. "Just trying to help you stay calm through the storm."

As if to prove his point, Hazel jumped at another rumble of thunder. For once, she was grateful for the distraction. She knew there was nothing real between them, in fact, she had been reminding herself of it daily, but hearing Nelson so readily agree with her words hurt worse than she thought it would.

Nelson sighed at her jumping and crawled over her sleeping bag. "Scoot over," he said curtly.

Uh, oh. What did I do now? "Okay..." She scooted over and Nelson planted himself next to her. Once settled, he wrapped his strong arms around her and tucked her into his chest. *Oh, good gracious. Will miracles never cease?*

She could hear Nelson mutter something under his breath, but she couldn't make out what it was. Snuggling further into his warm and protective embrace, she tilted her chin up a bit. "What was that?"

"Nothing. Just wondering why you're scared of storms." Nelson's voice sounded strained and Hazel wondered if she should pull away.

Maybe he's getting tired of helping me. He's certainly been my hero all week, I'll bet he's glad it's almost over. She chewed her lip as she thought about his curiosity. Finally, deciding it wouldn't matter if she told him because the likelihood of her ever seeing him after this trip was slim, she opened her mouth. "When I was little, there was a really big storm, thunder, lightning, hard rain, you name it. It was an epic storm."

"Worse than this one?" Nelson mumbled against her head.

"Way worse. The thunder hadn't really stopped rumbling by the time another would pick up. It seemed like daytime there was so much lightning. Just crazy. And it was raining so hard that the rain was literally bouncing off the ground."

Nelson grunted.

"Anyway, we were all gathered in the family room reading, because our electricity was out when lightning struck about a hundred feet from the house."

Nelson stiffened and pulled her out a little from his body so he could look in her face. "Really?"

Hazel nodded. "Yeah. It was crazy. I thought my eardrums had burst, it was so loud, and our tiny little home shook like an earthquake. The windows rattled, and I worried they would shatter."

"Whoa..." Nelson tucked her back under his chin and Hazel willingly burrowed in.

"The air was so static that it felt as if it were shocking you. Little crackles floated around our property for several seconds after the strike."

"Did it set anything on fire?"

"No. Things were probably too wet, but also, it actually hit the ground, not a tree or anything. We had a big black mark on the grass."

"That's nuts." Nelson shook his head.

"I know." She let her fingers play with the buttons on his plaid shirt. "And I've been scared of storms ever since. I know it's stupid. Odds of being near another strike are slim to none, but I can't seem to help it. It's become a conditioned response."

Nelson nodded. "It's no wonder. I've never heard of someone being that close to a strike. I mean, you hear of stuff in the news, but to actually meet someone that's experienced it is different." He wrapped his arms tighter around her and Hazel let herself pretend that it was because he wanted to protect her.

"At least no one was hurt. We were all frightened, but fine. No biggie. And as far as I know, I'm the only one who's still a fraidy cat about the whole thing."

"Well, that's good, I suppose." Nelson chuckled, and the sound rumbled against Hazel's cheek. "I guess that gives you something to write in your books about, huh? You can put in a lightning strike and let the guy save the girl."

If only, if only. "Yeah... a storm would make a great romantic scene."

CHAPTER 12

The next morning dawned grey and wet. Hazel fumbled with her poncho as she tried to pull her head through the correct hole. "They should have taken non-coordinated people into consideration when they created these things," she whined, pulling her head back out of yet another arm hole.

Finally, she managed to get the blasted thing situated and then spent several moments peeling the plastic away from her clothes, trying to get it to lay right so she would be as dry as possible.

Climbing out of her tent, she glanced toward the fire pit. The crew had managed to start a blaze this morning and Hazel was extremely grateful. She glanced at all the brightly colored heads of her fellow campers. *Now this is Pacific Northwest weather.* It wasn't raining exactly, it was misty. It was as if the very air were made up of floating bits of water, and after last night's rain, everything was soaked and cold.

With a shiver, Hazel wrapped her arms around herself and walked over to the cheery flames. Standing in front of the pit, she put her hands out, reaching for the warmth it offered.

"Did you sleep okay last night?" Jack popped up at her side and Hazel jumped a little.

"Oh! Yeah, thanks." She gave him a small smile, then took a subtle side step to put more distance between them.

"That rain was crazy, huh?" He grinned at her as he held out his hands as well. "We ended up sleeping almost on top of each other to keep from touching the sides of the tent."

Hazel frowned. *That had to be awkward.* "Um. Why would it matter if you touch the sides of the tent?"

Jack raised his eyebrows. "If you touch the side of a tent, it lets the moisture in. We would have been soaked."

"Oh..." Hazel's eyes darted back to the fire. *Boy was I lucky. How in the world did I not screw that one up?*

"In fact," Jack looked around before nodding his head toward the family of four, "they ended up with a bunch of water last night. The crew had to set them up a new tent and everything."

"Oh, wow. I had no idea."

"It had nothing to do with someone touching the side," Nelson's annoyed voice popped up behind her. "Good morning, Beautiful," he said softly before kissing her cold cheek. "There was a tear in the tent that we didn't know about. But we got them taken care of."

Hazel suddenly felt quite warm, despite the coolness of the morning. Looking over her shoulder she asked, "Did you have to do that after you left last night?"

"What do you mean after he left?" Jack's voice had dropped and both Nelson and Hazel whipped their heads toward him.

"I took her dinner last night, just like I did to the rest of the group," Nelson growled. "Not that it's any of your business."

Jack scowled right back. "Of course it's my business. People like you think you can take advantage of the rest of us." Jack pushed Hazel behind him and stood toe to toe with Nelson. "She might not be able to see past the dollar signs, but I can. And there is nothing about your money that gives you the right to take advantage of someone."

Hazel was shocked. Quickly, she stepped around Jack and came to the side of the two men, but she had no idea how to handle the situation in front of her. *Why do I always freeze when it comes to confrontation?* She reached out and gave Jack's arm a little shake. "Jack, nothing happened. Please stop." Her voice didn't carry over the threats the two men were throwing at each other, but Hazel couldn't bring herself to be any louder. It was as if her voice was in a vice and she had no control.

Suddenly a loud, ear-cracking whistle rent the air. All three of them turned toward the sound and Hazel cringed, putting her hands on her ears.

"Knock it off, you jerks," Mallory said with her hands on her hips. Storming over, she used her finger to point from one man to the other. "Your neanderthal tactics are ruining the camping trip for everyone else and scaring Hazel, to boot."

Both men looked over at Hazel to see her cringing away from the situation. Nelson's chin fell to his chest and even Jack looked a little contrite.

"You two need to knock it off." Mallory continued in her scolding. "Nelson, you should know better than to get into a fight, I mean, come on, you're the one in charge here, even if Jack is being a jerk."

"Hey-" Jack started.

"And you should know better than to continue to hit on a girl who's taken," Mallory interrupted him. Stepping forward, she poked him in the chest. "Hazel has told you over and over again that she's with Nelson and if that wasn't enough, her body language screams she's not interested. But you just keep trying and it's driving the rest of us crazy."

Jack's jaw dropped, but nothing came out of his mouth.

Hazel bit her lip to keep from smiling. This teenage girl was taking these grown men to task, and it was fantastic. *I would have never thought Mallory would be so helpful.*

"So, are you two ready to call a truce?" Mallory's hands were back on her hips. "Or should I continue to insult you guys until I burst those dumb egos?"

Nelson snorted and gently pushed his fist into Mallory's shoulder. "Nope. You're right. My ego can't take any more." He smiled wide and put a hand out to Jack. "Truce?"

Jack continued to glare at Nelson and Mallory while Annette slipped up to the group. "Come on, Jack," she said soothingly. "Nelson has treated Hazel like a princess all week. You really need to let it go."

Blowing out a long breath, Jack ran a hand through his hair. "Fine. But that doesn't mean I have to be happy about it." He reached out and the two men gave a couple of hard shakes.

For a moment it looked as if they would continue to hold on to each other's hands and Hazel worried that it was all still a show, but eventually they let go.

"Great!" Mallory clapped her hands. "Nothing like squeezing each other's hands to death to see who the winner is." She rolled her eyes and started to step away.

"Woot, woot!" Luke hollered. "Way to tell it like it is!" He started clapping and the rest of the camp joined in, shouting words of encouragement at Mallory.

Mallory grinned and did an elaborate bow, loving all the attention. "Thank you, thank you! I'm here until tomorrow!"

Annette slipped her arm through Jack's. "Come on, Big Guy. There are other available girls here, you know."

Jack grinned down at her and let Annette lead him toward the breakfast table.

Hazel watched the group move with awe. *How do they do that? How in the world do they have the courage to stand up and say what they want no matter the consequences? I mean, I can write about it, but in real life? Not happening.*

A throat cleared behind her and she turned to see a sheepish Nelson. His hands were stuffed in his pockets and a half grin graced his face. "Hey, Haze. I'm sorry. Mallory was right. I was out of line this morning. Forgive me?"

Hazel held in her sigh of pleasure. *I could look at that cute face all day.* Instead, she shrugged, feigning nonchalance. "Yeah. It's okay. I know you were just trying to protect me." She glanced around before leaning close to Nelson and whispering. "I'm really sorry this has all gotten so out of hand. I had no idea Jack would be so persistent. I mean, I've never had anyone pursue me at all, let alone so hard when they thought I was with another guy." Hazel scrunched up her face. "I feel bad that you've had to play hero to me all week." Her eyes dropped to the dirt, and she dug at it with her shoe.

Nelson's warm fingers touched the bottom of her chin and brought her face and gaze up to his. "I'm not sorry. You are one of the sweetest, most pure people I've ever met. It has been an honor to be yours this week."

This week. This week. The words floated through her head. *Well, at least I know where he stands. Nothing like reminding me this will end tomorrow to put me in my place.* She nodded and forced a smile. "Right. Well, thank you. I've really appreciated it."

Nelson frowned slightly, but didn't comment on her reaction. "Okay, ready for breakfast then? You're gonna need your energy today."

Hazel took his offered hand and began walking toward the line of people. "Yeah? What's on the agenda for today?" She savored the touch of his strong fingers and warm skin. *Tomorrow we go home and I'll never get to do this again. It's so unfair that I meet someone like him, someone just like what I've always dreamed of, and I have to let them go.*

Nelson looked over and pumped his eyebrows at her. "Repelling."

Hazel stopped in her tracks. "Repelling? Like, actually going down the side of a mountain?"

Nelson nodded, his expression was clearly excited, but Hazel couldn't muster up the same enthusiasm. *I'm the biggest chicken of all chickens. How in the world am I going to do this?*

Nelson nudged her shoulder. "Come on! It'll be fun! Just another new experience to write in your books about."

Hazel straightened her shoulders and nodded. "You're right. I came here to break out of the mold and I'm going to break out of the mold." She nodded again. *And hope I don't die in the process.*

NELSON BIT HIS LIP to keep from laughing. It was clear that Hazel was terrified, but he had to give her credit. She was working hard not to give in to the fear, but her shaking limbs, pale skin and sweating brow were dead giveaways.

"Hey, come on now," Nelson said with a grin. "No being scared. You're gonna love it!" He ducked his head so he could look her in the eye. When he finally had her attention, he straightened and put his hand on her shoulders. "Do you really think I would let you do something you might get hurt at?"

Hazel's wide, frightened eyes glanced down at the small cliff side she would be going down and then back up at him. "Are you telling me that if I fell I wouldn't get hurt? Because I don't think you're correct."

Nelson smiled reassuringly. "No. If you fell, you would definitely get hurt, but!" He put a finger up to stop her retort. "But I won't let you fall."

Hazel pinched her lips between her teeth and her eyes wandered down the cliff again.

"Hazel, look at me." Nelson waited until she obeyed. "I. Will. Not. Let. You. Fall. You got that? I haven't played lover boy all week just to let something happen to you now. Me and my crew know what we are doing. I promise. No one is going to get hurt. I would not bring anyone on a trip where I couldn't assure their safety." When she didn't look convinced, he tried speaking to her logical side. "Think about it, Haze. What kind of businessman would I be if I risked people's lives right and left? Hmm? I have these specific activities because we are capable of handling them. Nothing is going to happen to you."

Hazel gulped and nodded. "Okay," she said in a small voice. "I trust you."

Nelson couldn't help the way those three simple words sent him straight into the clouds. Hazel was absolutely terrified. In fact, she thought she was risking her very life by being here, but she trusted Nelson to take care of her. *No one ever trusts me with anything. At least, not so openly. How am I going to let her go tomorrow?* He cleared his throat to get rid of the sappy thoughts. "I promise not to break that trust. Now... ready?"

Hazel followed him to the edge where he had her turn away from the view and looked at him. "Now, you're just going to lean back and step down. It will be just like walking backwards. No big deal at all."

She nodded her head rapidly and her eyes darted to the ground.

"Nope. Eyes up here. Just look at me and start to move your feet."

"Come on, Hazel! You can do it!" Mallory shouted from below. She had been one of the first ones to climb down, hooting and hollering the whole way.

"See?" Nelson smiled. "Everyone knows you can do it. Now, just keep your eyes on me and lean back. Daniel and I have you."

Hazel seemed frozen and her breath was coming faster and faster. Nelson could see that if he didn't do something, she was going to hyperventilate and freak out. *I have to get her to relax a bit, but how?* A thought popped into his head and without worrying about it further, he stepped forward and grabbed the back of her head, kissing her soundly. It took a second, but he felt her muscles ease under the touch.

Slowly, he pulled back. "Better?" he asked quietly.

Hazel took a slow, deep breath and nodded. "Yes. Thank you. Unless that was meant as a final farewell."

Nelson stepped back and laughed. "There's the witty girl I've come to know." He smiled and nodded. "Now lean back," he said softly.

Hazel kept her eyes trained on his as she slowly followed his commands. Her stare was intense and for a moment, Nelson forgot what he was doing. Her eyes were as blue as the sky that had come in after the misty haze had burned off that morning. The entire world had seemed brighter from the rain the night before and Hazel's eyes were a perfect match.

Mentally, he shook himself. *You've got a job to do, Bud.* "That's it. You're doing great. Good, a little further. Awesome." He smiled wide. "Perfect. Now start stepping down."

Hazel's foot moved, but the rest of her didn't and she jerked her head toward her foot in confusion.

"Nope. Up here, Babe. That's it. Remember you have to let out the rope with your right hand."

Hazel blew out a breath. "Oh, yeah. Got it."

Inch by inch, she started letting rope slide through her gloved hand and her body started to slip further down.

"Now, move your feet with the rope," Nelson quickly reminded her.

Hazel nodded. Her nosed scrunched up as she concentrated, but every inch she moved seemed to bring her more confidence.

Nelson watched, fascinated as he watched her get a hold of herself and let self-determination take over. Her foot movements were jerky at first, but by the third or fourth step, they started to be more smooth. *She's amazing.*

Halfway down, she started to move a little faster and a small grin spread across her face.

"That's it! Way to go, Hazel!" Mallory and Annette shouted their encouragement. Several of the others joined in and soon Hazel's small grin was a wide smile.

After several minutes, she got close enough to jump the remaining distance to the ground. Once she was steady on her feet, she raised her arms in the air and cheered. Daniel quickly raced forward and began helping her unbuckle all the equipment.

As soon as she was free, Mallory and Annette grabbed her and did that jumping hug thing that teenage girls seem to be fond of.

Nelson watched with a silly grin on his face from the top of the small cliff. But when Jack moved in to give her a hug, Nelson felt himself go on alert. Not letting go, Jack sent his gaze up to Nelson and winked at him.

Nelson felt his fists clench and jealousy roared through him. *If he doesn't let go now we're going to see if you can really die by jumping down this thing.*

Luckily, Mallory pulled her out of Jack's arms and moved Hazel over to the side so they could prepare for the last couple of campers to go down. *Thank you, Mallory.* Nelson ran his fingers through his hair. *Dude, I totally owe those girls. They haven't been what I expected, at all.*

"Alright, Bud." Nelson turned to Luke. "Time to go." Nelson got the teenage boy all hooked up and guided him down the wall.

It was another half hour before Nelson was able to get himself to the bottom. When it was his turn, he hooked up, called to Daniel that he was ready, and leapt off the edge.

"Whoo, hoo!" he shouted, one fist in the air as he reached the bottom in only a couple of jumps.

He quickly unhooked and gave Daniel a high five.

"Oof!" He was nearly bowled over as a body slammed into him. Nelson looked down and realized Hazel had wrapped herself around him and was squeezing tight. He was no dummy; he wrapped his arms around her and enjoyed holding her, even as he found himself curious as to why she had thrown herself at him. *Not that I'm complaining, but... she's not usually like this.*

Hazel finally pulled back and her gaze worked its way all over his face. "Are you okay?"

Nelson scrunched his eyebrows. "Am I okay? Yeah. I'm fine. Why wouldn't I be?"

Hazel's lips pinched into a thin line and she punched him in the shoulder. "You scared me to death, leaping off the edge like that! Don't you have any sense of self preservation?"

Nelson burst out laughing. "I've got enough. Besides," he wrapped an arm around her shoulder and began walking toward the rest of the group, "I think you have enough of that for the both of us."

Hazel rolled her eyes and shook her head. "You're crazy."

Nelson nuzzled the side of her head. "Yeah, but you love it," he teased. He felt Hazel tense under his arm and immediately wanted to slap himself, but there was no way to take the words back.

After a moment, Hazel shrugged. "I'll just let you believe that."

Nelson chuckled again, glad she hadn't called him out for using the 'L' word. *That was close.* The word had just slipped out. Laughing and teasing with her felt so natural and Nelson wasn't sure how he was going to handle it when she went home tomorrow.

Best not to think about it. It's not like I'm looking for anything long term, anyway. Remember, now is my time to shine. My brothers are out and I'm still free. No tying myself down.

Nelson said the words over and over to himself, but somehow, they felt more hollow than before. The idea of being footloose and fancy free wasn't nearly as appealing as it had been before he met Hazel.

CHAPTER 13

The time had finally come. The trip was over and they were heading back to the resort. Hazel couldn't help the feelings of melancholy and depression that were running through her. "I will not miss the mosquitoes," she grumbled as she stuffed her things into her bag, "but leaving Nelson?" She sighed. "How often do we get to meet the perfect book boyfriend in real life?" She started rolling up her sleeping bag. "Real life sucks. In a book, Nelson would be in love with me and we wouldn't have to leave each other."

She pursed her lips and tilted her head for a moment. "I can just see it now. When we go to say goodbye, I'd actually have the courage to say something. I'd admit how my feelings are real and are no longer fake. I'd be brave enough to reach out and kiss him, and in the middle of the kiss, he'll take over, letting me know that he feels the same way. And after we've kissed for a really long time," she grinned, "he'd pull back and say he can't handle my leaving. Will I please stay with him? Hmmm..." she narrowed her eyes, "maybe he would even ask me to marry him?"

She tilted her head back and forth. "That might be a little fast. But at least there would be a romantic spiel and he would admit he loves me and we would turn our fake relationship into a real one and *eventually* end up married." Hazel sighed and sat dejectedly on the ground, tears pricking her eyes. "Life is so unfair... Sheesh, I sound like a teenager."

She gave a watery chuckle and shook her head. Wiping the stray tear that had dribbled down her cheek, she finished packing her things and headed out of her tent.

The entire camp was a hive of activity. Workers dashed here and there, helping people put their packs on their four-wheelers and taking down tents and tarps. Hazel's eyes immediately found Nelson. He was laughing with Luke as they took down the large tent the teenage boy's family had been sleeping in.

Luke was smiling and telling Nelson a story and kept dropping the tent because he used his hands so much while he talked, but Nelson didn't say a word about it, just kept plugging away while enjoying Luke's words.

Hazel shook her head. *How can anyone help but love him?* She froze. *Oh my gosh, I think I do. I'm falling in love with this guy.* She closed her eyes tightly. *Great. I'm not so sure my readers will appreciate a book about unrequited love. Romances are supposed to have happy endings.*

Shoving her problems aside, Hazel started to take her stuff over to the ATVs. Before she could get there, Daniel bounded to her side and took hold of her duffle.

"Can't let the boss's girl carry her own stuff," he said with a teasing wink.

Hazel's cheeks heated up, and she gave a small, forced smile. *Except I'm not really his girl.* "That's very sweet of you, thank you, Daniel," she said instead.

Daniel lowered his voice. "Don't worry. It'll all work out."

Hazel frowned and cocked her head. *What is he talking about?* She gasped. *Does he know that it was all fake?* Embarrassment flooded her whole body and the blush that was on her cheeks now felt as if it would consume her.

Daniel chuckled and walked away, leaving Hazel to enjoy her mortification in peace.

Pinching her lips together, she walked back to her tent. Putting her hands on her hips, she eyed the thing, wondering how to start trying to take it down.

"Did you figure out the great mystery that is tent disassembling?" Nelson's voice rumbled in her ear.

Hazel jumped at his sudden appearance and put her hand to her heart. *Good thing this guy can't read minds.* "Nelson, you startled me!" she scolded.

Nelson grinned unrepentantly, then leaned in and kissed her cheek. "Morning, Beautiful."

Dang that stupid blush, she thought as heat once again flooded her face. *Why can't this be real?* "Good morning," she murmured in return.

Nelson reached out and ran a finger down her warm cheek. "You almost live in that color."

Hazel laughed uncomfortably and tucked a piece of hair behind her ear. "Yeah. Between embarrassing easily and having fair skin, I was doomed from the start."

"It looks good on you," Nelson said, a smile still on his face.

The sincere comment only made Hazel's blush fire up even more. She put her cool hands on her cheeks, attempting to bring her skin under control, but to no avail. *I'm a total lost cause. I create happy endings for other people, but I can't get one for myself. Stinky, stink, stink... stinkin'.*

Nelson laughed and reached out to take her hand. "Come on, let's get this tent folded up."

They stepped up to the structure and Hazel poked at it. "Are you sure this thing will fit inside that?" She pointed at the small bag lying next to them.

"Yep!" Nelson grinned. "It's really not as hard as it looks."

Hazel nodded and pursed her lips. "Alrighty, then. Show me what to do."

NELSON WALKED UP BEHIND Hazel as she crouched down to pull up the stakes.

"Sheesh. What did you do?" Hazel grunted as she tried to pull up the plastic piece. "Dig these in with a jack hammer?"

Nelson laughed then leaned over and wrapped his arms around her, gripping the stake as well. He felt her stiffen under him, but couldn't bring himself to pull away. *After today, I won't see her again. No one can blame me for taking every opportunity left, right?*

It only took a minute for Hazel to relax in his arms and Nelson felt a measure of relief that she hadn't pushed him away. "Can I help you?" he asked in her ear.

"S-sure," she stammered breathily.

Nelson held in his smirk at her reaction. *It really is too bad I'm not looking to settle down at the moment. I think I could fall into serious like with her if I wasn't careful.* "Alright, here we go." Nelson gave a firm yank, pulling out the stake, but sending Hazel off balance. She fell backwards, straight into him, causing them both to fall on their backsides.

"Oh my gosh, I'm so sorry," Hazel said quickly, attempting to scramble to her feet.

Nelson laughed and wrapped his arms around her waist before she could get up. "I probably should apologize, since that was my fault, but I'm not really sorry at all," he teased in her ear.

Hazel's breathing was fast and shallow and Nelson loved that he had that affect on her.

"Ready to grab the next one?" Nelson asked.

Hazel nodded, but didn't speak.

Once he let her go, she darted up and wiped the dirt off her tush. "Good thing we're headed back today," she muttered. "I probably stink like a grizzly bear who just woke from hibernation."

Nelson laughed again. "Hazel, you are a riot. Where do you come up with these things? And why would a hibernating bear smell different than a regular bear?"

Hazel grinned back at his reaction. "Well, I'm a writer. It's my job to come up with quippy responses. I just usually keep them to myself."

She narrowed her eyes. "You have the uncanny ability to bring them out of me."

Nelson finished dusting off his pants and took a bow. "It's a gift."

Hazel nodded and raised her eyebrows. "Very nice. As for the bear, one that's been hibernating won't have bathed in a long time. Or at least won't have gotten in the water in a long time." She shrugged. "Truth be told, they probably all stink, just like me."

Nelson chuckled and walked over to the next spike. "Come on, the group is going to be waiting for us if we don't get a move on."

Hazel huffed, but followed him and together they pulled up the rest of the stakes without any more incidents.

Nelson patiently showed Hazel how to remove the poles and fold them up. Then they rolled up the tent and stuffed it inside its bag.

"We don't need to get too technical with it, because my crew is just going to take it out and clean it when we get back. So, this is fine," he grunted as he stuffed the last of the nylon fiber into the duffle.

Hazel stood and dusted off her hands. "Great! We did it!"

Nelson hefted the bag over his shoulder. "Looks like it's time to head back. You ready?"

Hazel looked around at the empty campground and nodded. "Yeah. It was great and definitely a new experience for me, but yeah. I'm ready to go de-stinkify."

Nelson made a face. "Is that a word?"

Hazel winked as she walked to the ATVs. "Author's license."

Shoot, I'm going to miss that girl. Laughing, he picked up his pace and caught up with her.

Several hours later, the whole crew arrived back at the castle with a sigh of relief. Nelson was ready for not only a shower, but a break from babysitting so many people. *Especially Jack,* he thought sourly. *If I never see that jerk again, it will be too soon.* Thoughts of Jack brought him back to thoughts of Hazel, and his heart clenched. *Now that one, I'm going to miss.*

Shoving his melancholy thoughts aside, Nelson walked out in front of the barn and waited for the campers to follow.

"Thank you all for coming!" he called out with a loud voice. A couple of whoops rang through the air and Nelson grinned. "I hope you all had a good time and enjoyed getting away from life for a bit. If you'll gather your luggage and head inside, I'm assuming you remember that a final night in the castle is part of your package. So enjoy your warm showers and a good meal and be safe on your travels tomorrow." He put up his hand. "Thank you!"

The group surged forward and everyone took turns slapping Nelson on the back or giving him a hug.

"We had such fun!" Mallory squealed, gripping Nelson in the tightest hug he'd ever had.

Who knew a tiny thing like her was so strong? Nelson was grateful to the teenager for her moxy and interference with Jack and Hazel. Especially since Jack only seemed to get worse when Nelson was around.

"I'm glad you had fun. And thank you for watching out for Hazel," Nelson said as he awkwardly patted the girl on the back.

Mallory stepped back and gave him a bold wink. "It was a pleasure to be here." She grinned, put her arm through Annette's and they bounded off to gather their things. Annette barely had time to wave at Nelson before Mallory had dragged her away.

Nelson closed his eyes and chuckled, thoroughly amused by the young girls' enthusiasm.

"My man!" Luke spread his arms wide and wrapped them around Nelson with a couple of loud slaps on the back. "Dude, for a billionaire, you're pretty awesome!"

Nelson's eyebrows shot up while he held his breath. During the week, the longer they kept Luke away from his phone, the more outgoing he had become and the more his growing teenage body had begun to smell. *Guess once social media was gone he had to have some other kind of outlet. Now, if we could just get him to use a little more deodorant.*

Soon everyone was gone except for Jack and Hazel, who stood talking off to the side. Nelson felt his fists clench and had to keep from storming over to rip her away from the guy, but resist he did. *She doesn't look upset. Maybe she's okay.*

But when Jack reached out and touched Hazel's arm, Nelson couldn't take it any longer. His muscles were tight and his chest puffed out as he stalked over, easily slipping his arm around Hazel's shoulders. "Everything alright, Sweetheart?" he asked quietly in her ear, then left a kiss on the side of her head.

His tension completely melted when she beamed up at him. "Yeah, thanks. Everything's fine."

"Hey, Man." Jack caught Nelson's attention and held out a hand. "No hard feelings?"

Nelson glared at Jack's face, then his hand, then back at his face. He didn't move until Hazel jabbed him in the gut with her elbow.

"No hard feelings," Nelson forced out and took the proffered peace offering.

Jack let go of Nelson's hand and laughed uncomfortably while running his hand through his hair. "Yeah, I was just apologizing to Hazel. I was a jerk this week and after Mal's little tirade, I stepped back to have a good look at things." He blew out a breath. "It was easy to see how much you guys like each other, and I shouldn't have tried to interfere." He stuffed his hands in the front pockets of his cargo shorts and kicked at the dirt.

"Yeah. Well." Nelson cleared his throat. "It's cool. No harm done."

Jack nodded and gave a half grin. "Great. I guess I'll... see you around?"

Hazel smiled and gave a small wave. "See ya," she said softly.

Nelson kept his arm around Hazel as they watched Jack strut up to the castle. "I did not see that coming," Nelson finally said into the silence.

Hazel began giggling. "Me either. I mean, first Mallory with her little, mama tiger personality, then you looked like you might pass out when Luke hugged you. And now Jack apologized." She looked up at Nelson, her eyes dancing. "I think everyone must be a little loopy from sleeping on the ground all week. Or... maybe someone found some special mushrooms we don't know about."

Nelson chuckled and pulled Hazel into his chest. "Something set them off, that's for sure." He pulled back and studied Hazel's content expression. *I'm not ready for her to go. But I can't ask her to stay. That would definitely send the wrong message. This was supposed to be totally fake and I'm not in the market to settle down.*

Nelson opened his mouth with every intention of saying goodbye, so he was just as shocked by his next words as Hazel appeared to be. "Can you stay a little longer?" *Wait. What? Where the heck did that come from?*

Hazel's jaw dropped. "Um... I don't understand."

Neither do I. "Uh..." Nelson let go of her and tugged at his shirt collar. "I mean, I was just thinking. You know... you came on this trip to kind of break out of your comfort zone and experience more things for your books. Maybe if you, um... had a little more time, I could take you on another adventure. You know, help you gain more material for your writing." Nelson's eyes were everywhere but on Hazel. *I can't believe I just said all that. She's going to think I'm nuts. First, I force her into a fake relationship, even if it was for her protection, and now I'm trying to get her to stick around. She's going to think I'm just like everyone else, totally taking advantage of her kindness.* "You know, just as friends," Nelson hurried to blurt out. "I mean, with Jack gone, there's no pressure to have to perform for anyone anymore."

Nelson finally managed the courage to look at Hazel's face. He wasn't sure what to think when he noticed she appeared stoic.

"Oh, yeah. Um... no pressure." She nodded calmly. "That actually... well that would be great. I'm sure my readers will love it." She turned and took a couple of steps toward the castle. Pausing, she spoke over her shoulder. "What exactly did you have in mind?"

Nelson rubbed his chin, trying not to appear too eager. *Friends. Just friends, Dude. You're just helping her break out of her shell.* "Let me think on it. Can I meet you for breakfast tomorrow in the restaurant and we'll get it figured out?"

"Sure." Hazel watched her toes as she kicked at the dirt. "See you then."

"Sounds good. See ya." Nelson watched her walk away. As excited as he was to have her stick around for a bit, there was something in her expression that gave him pause. *She's probably worried about hurting my feelings. She only thinks of me as a friend and is worried that she'll have to let me down.* Nelson's heart fell at the thought. *I guess I'll just have to make sure she understands I'm not on the market, anyway. I'm sure that will help her feel better.*

CHAPTER 14

Hazel wasn't sure if she should be excited or brokenhearted. One part of her was thrilled that Nelson had offered to take her on another adventure. The other part was depressed that he had made it very clear their fake relationship was over.

Luckily, her confusion hadn't affected her sleep. After arriving in her gorgeous hotel room, she had promptly stepped into the shower, not emerging for an hour. Once dressed, she had climbed under the covers and stayed there until morning. *Just goes to show how tired I was,* she mused.

"I wonder what we're going to do?" Her nose crinkled as she contemplated what the future held. "He said he wanted to do something that was out of my comfort zone. But what exactly did he have in mind?" She plopped on the bed. "Hopefully nothing death defying." She huffed a laugh and stood up. "That would be just like Nelson."

Humming a little tune under her breath, she finished getting ready and headed down to Hayden's restaurant. For the first time in days, Hazel's hair fell long and soft over her shoulders and she had taken the time to put on makeup and some nice clothes. *I know it doesn't really matter, but just once it would be nice if Nelson could see me in something other than my camping grubbies.*

She shoved away the thought that she was trying to catch his attention. *Any girl would feel the same way. We all like to look our best,* she reassured herself. *Besides, Nelson made it very clear that we're just friends. Our fake relationship is over and he obviously had no desire to pursue anything real.*

The thought made her heart sink, but she thrust back her shoulders and refused to give into the feeling. "I'll take what I can get. It's not like there was ever really any hope, anyway. The man is so far out of my league it's not even funny."

"What's not funny?"

Hazel squeaked and spun around at the sound of the familiar voice. "Nelson! You jerk!" Hazel scolded. Stepping toward him, she socked him in the shoulder. "Stop doing that!"

"Ow!" Nelson feigned being hurt and put his hand on his shoulder. "Give a girl a shower and suddenly she gets violent. Maybe I should take you out and roll you in the dirt again, it might calm you down."

Hazel fought to keep from smiling. Instead, she raised an eyebrow at him. "I'd like to see you try it. Last night's shower was the best thing to happen to me in a long time."

Nelson's eyes twinkled with mischief and Hazel began to panic. *Oh, crud. What now?*

He stepped up close, his fresh smell penetrating her nose and discombobulating her senses. "Is that a challenge?"

"N-no," she stammered. "Why would that be a challenge?"

Nelson's eyes dropped from hers down to her lips and back up. "I enjoy getting clean as much as the next person, but if that's the best thing that's happened to you, then we need to broaden your horizons. Not to mention, I must not have done my job as your fake boyfriend very well."

Rather than the warm heat that usually hit Hazel, a fiery flame engulfed her, and she knew her cheeks were ablaze. "Uh..." She had no comeback. No quick quips, no flirtatious banter. Her author brain had completely shut down when she needed it most.

Nelson's lips twitched as he fought a smile. Lifting one finger, he ran it down her hot cheek. "Never play poker, Haze. You'll lose every time."

"So noted," she said weakly, her eyes still stuck on his dark ones.

Nelson laughed and stepped back, releasing her from the spell she had been under. "Ready to get some breakfast? We're going to need our energy today."

"You say that a lot. Why does that have to sound so ominous?" Hazel turned back toward the restaurant and began to walk with him

Nelson reached out and grabbed her hand like he had been doing all week. "I've got some major fun planned for us today," he said with a pump of his eyebrows.

Does he even know he's holding my hand? Or does he just treat all women like this? I'm so out of my league. "Aren't you going to give me any clues?"

"Where's the fun in that?" Nelson laughed.

Hazel rolled her eyes. "Because then I'll be able to be prepared, duh."

"Again I say, where's the fun in that?"

Hazel sighed dramatically. "If you want me to chicken out before we even begin, then I guess surprising me is the way to go."

"Or, if I want you to be just fine until the last second, this is the way to go." Nelson dropped her hand to hold open the door to the restaurant. "I guess you're just going to have to trust me," he whispered in her ear as she passed him.

A shiver ran down Hazel's spine and she did her best to ignore it. *Just friends. Just friends.*

Warm, savory and sweet smells hit her as they entered the dining area. "Mmm..." she hummed. "Wow, that smells good."

"Yeah." Nelson took a big whiff. "Hayden's pretty darn amazing in the kitchen." He leaned in. "But don't tell him I said so. He's funner to rile than you are."

Hazel scowled. "I don't rile."

"I guess that's true. You get flustered. He gets angry. Either way, it's hilarious."

Hazel rolled her eyes playfully. "Come on, Mr. Instigator. I'm starving."

Nelson put his hand to his chest, grabbed her hand and walked to the hostess podium. "A woman after my own heart." He smiled at the young woman waiting for them. "Hey, Abigail! How's it going?"

"Good!" She chirped with a wide smile. "Two of you this morning?"

Nelson winked. "Yep. I starved this poor woman all week while we were camping and now I have to feed her to make up for it."

Abigail tsked her tongue and put a fake frown on. "You poor dear. Don't worry. Hayden's cooking will cheer you right up."

Hazel's stomach took that as a cue to growl loudly, causing her to gasp and put her hand over it. "I guess my stomach agrees with you."

Nelson cracked up, and the hostess giggled. "Right," she said. "Let's get you two seated."

Grabbing menus, Abigail took them into the beautiful restaurant and made sure they were settled in one of the private booths. "Trevor will be your waiter this morning. He'll be by shortly to take your drink orders."

"Thanks, Abby," Nelson called after her as she walked back to the front section. "I'd ask if you're ready to eat, but I think your stomach answered that question already."

Hazel scrunched up her nose. "Nothing like starting the day with an embarrassing situation. Gets the blood pumping."

Nelson laughed and shook his head. "Nice one." He drummed his fingers on the table top and Hazel looked up from the menu.

"Do you already know what you want?" she asked.

Nelson put his arms down and leaned across the table. "I've had just about everything on the menu. You really can't go wrong here. Want a recommendation?"

Hazel set the folder down and pursed her lips. "I don't know. How do I know I can trust what you're going to tell me? You won't even tell me what we're doing today."

Nelson smirked. "Nice try, but it won't work." He leaned back and folded his arms across his chest. "But when it comes to food, you can always trust me."

Hazel pointed a finger at him. "So you say, but all I have to go on is camping food, which was very good, but still isn't quite the same as restaurant food. Not to mention, Hayden made the camping food as well."

Nelson put his finger to his lips. "Shhh! No giving away my secret! I want the girls to think I cook all that myself. Gotta have something other than this pretty face to attract the ladies, you know."

Hazel felt a stab of jealousy at the thought of Nelson trying to impress other girls, but then she paused and thought about what he really said and her heart softened. "What do you mean you need something other than a pretty face? Nelson, you have lots of qualities girls are looking for."

The playfulness in Nelson's expression dropped, and he narrowed his eyes at her. "It's okay, I was already planning on buying your breakfast, Haze. You don't have to butter me up."

The joke fell flat when Hazel didn't laugh and the moment became awkward. *Do I just change the subject or try to figure out why he would say something like that? Maybe it's okay to push a little? It's not like we're going to be having anything long term between us. I mean, if he gets mad at me, it's not like we're neighbors or something.*

Taking a deep breath, Hazel firmed her resolve. Nelson sounded like he needed a friend and she was just the person to do it, even if it made her uncomfortable and wasn't even close to what she actually wanted with him.

"I wasn't planning on you paying for breakfast, Nelson. I'm here because I enjoy your company. As does everyone I've ever seen around you. And truth be told," she cleared her throat, "I'm pretty sure you don't need extra help attracting the ladies. You seem to do it naturally."

"Hey, folks," their waiter interrupted. "Nelson, my man! How's it going?" Trevor fist-bumped Nelson and nodded a greeting. "Good to see you here. And with a lady!" He winked at Hazel, bringing her blush to the forefront. "And a cute one at that. Nice choice, Man," he teased.

Nelson leaned back with a smirk on his face. "Eh, you know me Trevor. I never settle for anything other than the best."

Trevor laughed and nodded again. "Sounds about right. What can I get you two this morning?"

Nelson sent his dark eyes to Hazel's. "Mind if I order for us?"

Her heart picked up at the question. She knew that letting him order for her was not only a show of trust, but implied an intimacy that wasn't really there, but that she desperately wanted. "That would be wonderful," she said softly.

Nelson's eyes flashed before going back to their usual mischievous demeanor. "Alright." He rubbed his hands together. "We'll take two omelets, one with bacon and cheese and the other one with veggies. Give us two glasses of orange juice and two cinnamon rolls, plus a side of hash."

Hazel's jaw dropped.

"Gotcha. I'm on it." Trevor grinned and took off.

"That's a ton of food! I don't know if I can eat all that."

"That's why you have me." Nelson's lips pulled up in a half grin.

"Maybe we should just share a cinnamon roll," Hazel mused.

"No way! Are you kidding me? I do not share my pastries."

Nelson's face was so serious, Hazel couldn't help but burst out laughing.

NELSON LOVED WATCHING Hazel laugh. She was so quiet most of the time, but when she laughed, she completely let go. Her face lit up and the anxiety she held onto disappeared. Her already cute features transformed into something beautiful and Nelson found himself entranced.

"You don't share your pastries? Then what do you share?" Hazel said as she wiped tears of mirth from her cheeks.

Nelson scrunched his lips to one side and made a big deal out of thinking. "Well, I share my wonderful company. Isn't that enough?" He raised his eyebrows.

Hazel laughed again and Nelson wanted to pump a fist in the air, but he refrained. Barely.

When she had finally calmed herself back down, she smiled at him. "Are you really not going to tell me what we're doing today?"

"No way! I am not giving you any reason to chicken out."

"You're going to make me chicken out before we start!" She threw her hands up in the air, but her smile let him know she wasn't really going anywhere.

His eyes were drawn to her lips as she spoke and he found his temperature spiking as he thought about kissing them. *I don't have a good excuse now. Our fake relationship is over, so no more kissing.* He was surprised at how much that thought saddened him. *Just friends. Remember yesterday? She doesn't have any interest in you other than friends. Her face said it all.*

"Two orange juices. One for the lady and one for the dork."

"Watch it," Nelson growled. "I'm trying to impress her, Man. You're killing me here!'

Trevor laughed. "Sorry. I'll keep the truth to myself."

"Much appreciated."

Hazel grinned and watched the two men banter back and forth.

"Alrighty then, your meals will be out shortly. I think Chef Truman was handling them himself," Trevor stated.

Nelson froze. *Crud. If Hayden knows I have a girl here, he'll make a scene.*

"Really? Oh my gosh, that's so fantastic!" Hazel nearly squealed.

Her excitement melted away Nelson's fears. *She is so easy to please. But what if-* Jealousy ripped through Nelson and before he could stop it, words he never should have spoken burst out of his mouth. "You do know he's married, right?"

Hazel's eyes widened, and she blinked at him in surprise. "Of course. I'm just excited to be able to say I ate something he cooked personally." She tilted her head and Nelson had to look away from her blue eyes that saw too much. "I'm sorry. I guess some of us little people get excited about dumb things."

Nelson rubbed a finger on the wood grain of the table. "Nah. It's fine. I just wanted to make sure you didn't have a crush on him or something. You know, because his wife is pretty awesome and no offense, but she's like twice your size."

Hazel blushed and ducked her head. "Uh, no. He's not who I have a crush on. No worries there."

"Wait. Are you saying you do have a crush on someone?"

Hazel turned to look out at the dining area. "What makes you say that?"

Nelson pointed a finger at her. "The red covering your entire face and neck."

Hazel put her hands to her cheeks. "Maybe it's just being here with you," she said softly.

Nelson scoffed and shook his head. *Yeah right.*

Hazel frowned. "And just what is that supposed to mean? You never did answer my question from earlier. You always seem to make derogatory comments about yourself and I'm never sure if you really mean them or not."

Nelson gave her a sad smile. "That's because you see everything through rose-colored glasses. You write happy ever afters, remember? Life isn't like that."

"Pray tell, what's so wrong with you?"

Nelson studied her. *Does she actually care? I mean, I want her to, but...* Her bright, blue eyes never left his, and he finally shrugged, figuring it wouldn't hurt anything to tell her. *It's not like she's sticking around, anyway.* "I've just learned to accept the truth over the years."

"And what is that?"

"That I'm the overlooked Truman brother," Nelson stated matter-of-factly.

A cute, little V formed between Hazel's eyebrows and Nelson found himself wanting to use his thumb to smooth it out. His fingers twitched, and he forced himself to fold his arms over his chest. "Why do you feel overlooked?" she asked.

"I've always just kinda been the outcast, I guess. Eli, my oldest brother, has always been the responsible one. Like even when we were kids, he was always organized and planning things." Nelson raised an eyebrow. "He's still pretty bossy. I'm just better at not listening than I was as a kid."

Hazel laughed lightly, but her eyes were concerned. "And Hayden?"

"Oh," Nelson played with the silverware on the table, "Hayden has always had a chip on his shoulder. He was kinda a big kid, but then he started playing football and turned into a lady killer. My sisters are in a category by themselves, you know? Laken leaves a trail of broken hearts everywhere she goes and Teagan doesn't realize anyone exists outside of her plants."

"Well, well, well. What have we here?" A deep voice interrupted their conversation and Nelson had to refrain from rolling his eyes. *He just had to bust in. Now he's going to make a big deal out of the fact I have a girl here and probably send Hazel running.*

Hazel's eyes were wide as she took in Hayden. Nelson wasn't short, he was right around six feet, but his build was slimmer. He was built like an endurance athlete as opposed to Hayden's linebacker frame.

"Never thought I'd see the day my little brother would bring a girl home," Hayden smirked.

"Seriously?" Nelson scrunched up his face. "I didn't bring her home. I brought her to breakfast. Which you're supposed to be cooking, by the way."

Hayden waved off his comments. "Tomato, tomahto. And I've got James finishing up your food. It will be here shortly. Until then..." Hayden's smile was devious as he slid into Nelson's side of the booth.

"Hello. I'm Hayden Truman, this knucklehead's older and much smarter brother." Hayden reached his hand across the table.

Hazel smiled and her cheeks turned pink. "Hello. I'm Hazel."

"Hazel? Nice to meet you." Hayden leaned back and studied her. "And just how long have you and my bro here been dating?"

"Oh! No. We-"

"A week," Nelson interrupted. He immediately wanted to slap himself. *Why, oh why can't I keep my big mouth shut?*

Hayden went back and forth between Hazel and Nelson. "So, pretty new then. I guess I can forgive you for not introducing us before now."

"Like you're one to talk," Nelson mumbled. *Where the heck is our food? And since when did Hayden get so chatty?*

Hayden shook his head. "Whatever. You know mine and Cadence's relationship was different."

"Yeah, well, if you don't mind, I prefer spending time with pretty girls rather than ugly mugs like yours," Nelson snapped.

Hayden slowly turned his head and his mouth pulled up in a crooked grin. "You're awfully moody over there. What's the matter, Nellie? Don't like it when your brother pushes his way into your business?"

Karma is a pain in the backside. "Message received, now if you'll-"

"Here we are folks, nice and hot." Their waiter arrived just as Nelson was getting ready to sock his brother in the nose.

I'm sure the media would love that. He glanced over at Hazel, who had been completely silent ever since giving Hayden her name. She was sunk into the back cushion of her booth and a troubled expression sat on her face. *Shoot. I'm surprised she hasn't run away already. I'll be lucky if she's still my friend after this.*

The thought of Hazel leaving and never speaking to him again sent a sharp jolt to Nelson's chest. The beautiful, quiet woman had wormed her way under his skin and there didn't appear to be anything Nelson could do about it.

"I suppose I should let you two eat in peace," Hayden said, smiling at Hazel. "It was a pleasure to meet you, Hazel. I hope to see you around."

"Thank you, you too," Hazel said so quietly she could barely be heard over the sound of dishes being placed on the table.

Finally, everything was settled and all the extra people were gone. Multiple plates wafting with sweet and savory steam sat between them, causing Nelson's mouth to water. "So, what do you think?"

"It looks delicious. I can't wait to try it." Hazel's smile looked strained and Nelson's guilt shifted up a notch.

"It tastes better hot, so let's go ahead and dig in." Nelson pulled one of the plates toward himself and took a massive bite of omelet.

Hazel gave him an incredulous look. "How in the world did you fit that in your mouth? I have several brothers, but whoa... that was impressive."

Nelson choked a little as he laughed. He chewed and swallowed before he answered her. "My brothers say I never left my teenage years, so," he shrugged, "who knows?"

"Nothing wrong with being a kid at heart," Hazel said with a more genuine smile. Leaning over the table, she took a bite of the other omelet. "Mmm..." she moaned. "This is delicious."

"Told you my brother was the best. He might be a jerk sometimes, but he knows his way around the kitchen." Nelson leaned in and put his hand to the side of his mouth. "Under no circumstances should you ever tell him I said that though."

Hazel winked and gave him a salute since her mouth was full.

Their little banter had lightened the mood considerably and Nelson chuckled at her response to him. *Maybe we can still be friends after all.*

CHAPTER 15

Hazel's legs shook like a newborn fawn's. "We're doing what?" she squeaked.

"Hang gliding!" Nelson said with a broad smile. "I thought about just taking you horseback riding, but I figured if we were going to go out with a bang, we definitely needed something bigger than that."

Hazel forced a laugh, but it ended up sounding deranged rather than nonchalant. "Oh, yeah, I can... I can see your point."

Nelson started laughing and didn't stop. Bending over, he rested his hands on his knees while he laughed from deep within. Hazel was completely entranced by the sound. It was easy to see that Nelson was usually a happy guy, but seeing him laughing in such an uninhibited way warmed her from her toes to the top of her head.

Breakfast had nearly broken her heart, listening to him talk about how he felt like he didn't fit in with his family. She wished they hadn't been interrupted before she could have responded to him, but she didn't want to bring back up a sore topic. *I guess I'll just have to show him how special he is.* She gulped. *Starting with hang gliding.*

She put her hand to her stomach as it lurched at the thought of flying through the air. *Maybe eating such a big breakfast wasn't the best choice.*

"Ahh..." Nelson wiped tears from his eyes. "Your face was amazing. Never ever play poker, Sweetheart."

Hazel rolled her eyes. "Like I haven't heard that a thousand times."

Nelson chuckled again. "Okay, I've got a buddy meeting us at the rendezvous point. Let's hop in my truck and we'll go back to my house and grab the gear before taking off."

Hazel didn't speak as Nelson took her hand and directed her to his vehicle sitting outside the restaurant. His truck was huge with extra doors and a long bed and oversized tires. "Is it legal to drive monster trucks on the road?" Hazel asked as he opened her door.

Nelson once again burst out laughing. "Hazel... you're my favorite."

Her cheeks went up in flames and she forced herself to keep her attention on the truck as she grabbed the handle to pull herself in. *If only he really meant that.*

Once Nelson had popped in the other side and pulled them out of the parking lot, he started talking again. "I have to admit the truck was one of my splurges. I mean, I was excited about my house and all, but what I really wanted was a truck so I could haul all my gear."

Hazel watched Nelson drive down a small road that seemed to go further into the forest. "Do you have a lot of gear, then?"

Nelson shrugged. "I had quite a bit before we found the treasure, but mostly only portable stuff. I've always kind of been an outdoor enthusiast, so I've collected things over the years."

"Just for your own enjoyment? Or for other reasons?" Hazel kept finding her gaze traveling back to his handsome profile. He had one arm on the edge of the door and the other at the top of the steering wheel. The position showed off his strong arms and Hazel had to tamp down the urge to run her fingers along the muscles protruding from his forearms.

"Mostly for myself, but one of the jobs I've held the most over the years has been as an instructor."

"Ah." Hazel cleared her throat and forced herself to look away from the scenery inside the truck to the stuff outside. "That explains why you were so comfortable being in charge of a whole group on a week long camping trip."

Nelson chuckled as he pulled into the driveway of a massive log cabin.

"Holy…" Hazel ducked down so she could see the whole house through the windshield. "This is yours?"

"Yep." He threw the truck into park and pulled out the key. "I'm not really a fancy guy, but even I'll admit that suddenly having access to so much money has been fun." He opened his door. "Come on, I'll show you around before we grab the glider."

Hazel gulped as she opened the door and eyed the step down. Suddenly, a hand appeared in her vision. Grabbing it, she let Nelson help her onto the concrete. "Thanks," she murmured once her feet were firmly planted.

"No prob. Let's go inside." Nelson kept ahold of her and practically dragged her through his front door.

The inside was just as fabulous as the outside. The log beams gleamed in the morning sunlight pouring through the large windows on every wall. A massive television hung over an equally massive fireplace. Nelson's love of the outdoors was apparent in the decorations. A bench made of oars sat along one wall and his coffee table looked like a repurposed surfboard.

"This is gorgeous," Hazel whispered reverently. *It's so him. Open, cheerful and unpretentious.*

"It's home," Nelson said easily, but Hazel could see pride in his eyes as he looked around the space with her.

"What we need is in the barn, so we need to head out back."

"You have your own barn?" Hazel asked with a frown. "I thought you had a barn at the castle."

"I had them build me one here as well. The one at the castle is for the business. This one is for me." Nelson winked at her as he led her out a sliding glass door and onto a large patio.

The house was mostly surrounded by forest, but a space behind the massive home had been cleared out and a large red barn stood in stark contrast to the evergreen trees surrounding it.

Nelson let go of her hand to push open the door and Hazel immediately felt the loss. *Going home tomorrow is going to hurt so bad...* She kept her sigh to herself. *Research for a book. Remember this is all just research for a book.*

The lie didn't sit well in her chest, just as Nelson lying to his family earlier hadn't. But she wasn't sure what else to do. Nelson had completely stolen her heart this week with his kindness and patience. He was better than any book boyfriend she could ever have imagined for herself. But right now she was in a fake bubble, and tomorrow she would be back to real life. *And for the first time ever, you'll get to feel real heartbreak.* She blinked back tears. *Maybe that can be good research too.*

NELSON GRABBED THE large duffle with the harnesses and walked it over to Hazel's feet. ""Kay, we need this and one other thing." He walked back into the barn and hefted the rolled up glider wing. "Oof," he huffed as he shouldered it and started walking it toward the doors.

"Do you need some help?" Hazel's sweet voice floated across the space.

"Nah. But if you want to grab that duffle, it'll save me a trip." Nelson maneuvered his way through the doors and walked around the house in order to put his bundle in the truck.

He held back a laugh as he turned to watch Hazel trudging along behind him. The duffle was obviously heavy for her, but the determined look on her face let him know she didn't want him to help her.

"Thanks," he said as she dropped it at his feet.

"Whew! That was heavy!" Hazel put her hands on her hips and smiled up at him. Once again, Nelson found himself entranced with the blue color of her eyes. Having come from a family where they all had dark hair and dark eyes, the blue seemed like a breath of fresh air. *I wonder if her kids will have those eyes?* Nelson's eyes widened as he jerked at the thought. *Whoa. Why am I thinking of Hazel's kids? She doesn't have feelings for me that way at all. And I'm NOT looking to settle down!*

Hazel frowned. "I'm sorry. Did I do something wrong?" She looked down at the duffle and back up at him.

"No," he choked out. "Nothing wrong at all." He shook his head to clear it of the picture of a young girl with his dark hair and her bright blue eyes. *Shut up, shut up, shut up!* he screamed at his brain. Forcing himself to look away, he bent over and grabbed the duffle, then hefted it into the bed. "I'm glad you wore a jacket, because it's going to be windy where we're going."

"Oh." Hazel looked at her clothes. "Do I need to change?"

"Nah. You've got sneakers on and your jeans are fine." Nelson walked over and opened her door. "Let's go flying!"

He watched her gulp and slowly move in his direction. As she reached the truck, he saw her set her jaw and throw back her shoulders. "Right. Let's go flying." Reaching up, she grabbed the handle bar and climbed into his massive truck.

Nelson grinned and shook his head. *Gotta give her credit. She might be quiet, but she's willing to push through her fears.*

Nelson got into his own seat and backed out, heading back out of the forest to the main road.

After they had been driving for about fifteen minutes, Hazel broke the silence. "Can I ask you a question?"

"Shoot," Nelson responded. *Maybe it will distract me from watching the sun highlight your hair.*

"Why did you tell your brother we were dating?" Hazel kept her eyes on her hands, wringing them in her lap.

Ah, crud. I knew it upset her. "I... well." Nelson rubbed the back of his neck, keeping his eyes on the road. "I wasn't going to, but Hayden was kinda getting up in my face and ticking me off. It kinda just happened. I didn't want to look like such a loser in front of him, you know?"

He could feel Hazel's eyes on him. "Why would you look like a loser if we weren't dating?"

Nelson cleared his throat and put both hands on the wheel, straightening his arms and pushing back in his seat. "I told you I'm kind of the black sheep. I'm not like my brothers... or sisters for that matter. I didn't even finish college." *Good thing she doesn't have feelings for me or this would definitely be the end of it.*

"I still don't understand."

Nelson jerked to look at her for a moment. "They think I'm worthless. Hayden's always going on about how I can't hold down a job. I'm the only one without a degree. And now both of my brothers have found amazing women and settled down, while I still 'play for a living.'"

Hazel tilted her head and studied him. Her intense gaze caused the temperature in the truck to spike and Nelson tugged on the collar of his t-shirt. Reaching over, he fiddled with the air conditioner, blasting it straight into his face in an attempt to cool himself down.

"Wow. You're easy to talk to." Nelson gave an uneasy chuckle. "I actually haven't ever told anyone all that before."

"Do you want my opinion, or does just talking help?"

Nelson frowned. "What do you mean?"

"All of us have problems and insecurities in our lives." Hazel shrugged. "And often, it feels good to talk to someone about them. But some people just want a listening ear and some people want a returned opinion." She looked back at him again. "Which do you want?"

Nelson kept his eyes on the road while he pondered her question. "I... geez, I've never had anyone ask me that before."

Hazel smiled. "I'm fairly quiet, but observant in social situations. I've learned most people need someone to talk to and by keeping my mouth shut, they often share their stories with me."

"Do you ever write about any of them?"

Hazel laughed lightly. "I can't say nothing I've ever written wasn't inspired by things I've heard, but it's always been changed enough that no one would recognize it." She looked across the cab. "Does that make you uncomfortable?"

Nelson pursed his lips and shook his head. "Should it? Are you planning to write a character like me?"

"Maybe," she teased with a grin. "You'd make a pretty good book boyfriend. But aside from that, you never answered my question. Do you want my opinion or just my ear?"

"I think... I'd like to hear your opinion," he said slowly. *I hope I don't regret this. But maybe it will help me put my feelings to rest if she spells it out plainly.*

"I think you need to quit worrying about your brother's opinions and realize how special you are."

Nelson's jaw nearly dropped. "You think I'm special?" He narrowed his eyes and darted them toward her and back to the road. "You don't mean special in a weird way, do you?"

Hazel giggled. "No! You're an amazing man, Nelson Truman. And it makes me sad that you think you aren't. I don't believe you're as much of an outcast as you imagine. Being different from your siblings doesn't mean you don't belong. I mean, my mom has always referred to me as 'the dreamer' of our family. My feet were on the ground, but my head was always in the clouds," she tilted her head back and forth, "or a book."

Nelson huffed a laugh and grinned.

"We have every kind of personality available in my family. Most of my brothers are loud and obnoxious, the complete opposite of myself, but that just makes the family gatherings more fun. But that aside, you truly are amazing. You were kind, patient and so protective this week, I-I don't even know how to thank you." Hazel's cheeks fired up as she talked.

"You really see all that when you look at me? Not just a goofy loafer?" *There's no way she really means that, is there?*

Hazel tilted her head and dropped her shoulders. "Really! I wouldn't lie to you!" She socked him in the shoulder.

"Ow!" Nelson tried to hold back his grin as he held the spot on his arm. "You've got a mean right hook."

"Hardy-har-har. We both saw how strong I was trying to carry that duffle bag to your truck."

"Yeah, that was pretty pathetic." Nelson laughed when she socked him again. "Hey, I'm drivin' here!" he yelled out in a New York accent.

They both laughed and settled into a comfortable silence. Nelson tapped his fingers on the steering wheel as a thought popped into his head. He debated asking it, but pretty soon the words slipped out of his mouth, anyway. "So, you said I'd make a good book boyfriend. You going to write a book about us?"

"About us?" she squeaked.

A pit formed in Nelson's stomach. *Is it that horrible to think about? I know she only thinks of me as a friend, but is it so laughable to think of more? Me and my stupid mouth.*

Hazel cleared her throat. "Maybe it had crossed my mind," she whispered.

Nelson whipped his head in her direction. "Really? Like you and me?"

"Well, it probably wouldn't be exactly me and you."

Nelson frowned. "Why not? I thought you said I'd make a good book character."

"Yeah, you would. But someone like you needs someone different than me."

Nelson thought he detected a sad tone in her voice, but he brushed the thought aside. "Why would I need someone different?"

"You need a woman who can keep up with you. Someone who isn't scared of everything and has more experience in life." She rested her head on her hand while her elbow balanced on the window ledge.

"Oh." Nelson looked to her and back to the road several times. "I guess I hadn't thought of that." *Can't get much clearer than that, I suppose.* His chest felt like someone had decided to carve it up with a knife. *You weren't interested anyway, Nelson. Just drop it.* "Well, scared or not, you're gonna love hang gliding." Nelson forced his tone into his normal easy, charming self.

Hazel laughed, but it sounded forced. "You might have to give me a push, I'm terrified just thinking about it."

"Eh, don't worry, you're going to be riding with me. All you have to do is hold on and enjoy the view."

"We're riding tandem?" Hazel's eyebrows shot up.

"Yeah. Did you think you would be able to ride alone on your first try?"

Hazel gave a relieved laugh. "I don't know what I thought, but riding tandem makes so much more sense."

"I'm happy to have relieved some of your fears," Nelson said with a laugh.

"Oh, I'm still freaked out. But knowing I won't have to do much helps a lot."

"This way you can't back out. Once I have you strapped in, you're stuck with me." Nelson gave her a confused look when she muttered under her breath. "What was that?"

"Nothing... nothing at all," she said sweetly.

CHAPTER 16

"Are you sure this is safe?" Hazel's voice shook as she looked at the slew of straps attached to her and Nelson.

"Haze, do you really think I would bring you on something where I thought you would get hurt?" Nelson frowned at her over his shoulder.

"Probably not. But what if I annoyed you really bad this last week and you're out for revenge?" She couldn't seem to get her heartbeat under control and she felt like she might hyperventilate if she didn't calm down.

Nelson laughed. "Only in one of your books, Haze. Only in one of your books."

"Everything looks good, Man," Nelson's buddy called from where he stood holding onto the edge of the glider.

A strong gust of wind rocked them back and forth and Hazel squealed and ducked her head into Nelson's shoulder blade.

"Sweetheart, you're going to have to bring down the volume or I'll be deaf by the time we get back," Nelson said with a chuckle.

"Sorry. I'll do my best to be quiet."

Nelson's smile dropped. "Forget I said anything. You're quiet enough. If you wanna make noise, you make some noise, okay?"

What is that supposed to mean? "Uh, okay." She blinked a couple of times at his hard stare. *His eyes are so dark, it looks like they have no end. Why, oh why, can't I be the woman he needs?*

"Great! Now remember, where can you put your hands?"

"Um," Hazel glanced around. She was attached to the right of Nelson, just one step behind his shoulder. "Here," she put her hand on the strap behind his right shoulder blade, "and here." She put her other hand on the strap at her own right shoulder.

"Perfect. You have to leave them there. No grabbing at the glider or we'll be in trouble, 'kay?"

Hazel nodded. The thought of trouble made her mouth too dry to speak. *I can't do this. I have to get down.* Her eyes started darting around wildly in an attempt to figure out how to unstrap herself.

"Haze... Haze... Hazel!" Nelson shouted at her.

She jerked her attention to him.

"I got you, Babe. Everything is going to be fine. I know you're going to love this," he said in a soothing tone. "Just hang on and trust me, okay?"

Hazel forced her breathing to slow. She took in a couple of long breaths through her nose and pushed them out from her mouth. "Okay," she said softly. She wasn't sure it was loud enough for Nelson to even hear her, but he must have read the word on her lips because his smile widened and he turned to his friend.

"Let's go!" he shouted.

Before Hazel was ready, the glider shifted forward as Nelson took a couple of running steps. Her feet fumbled after him.

"Tuck 'em up!" Nelson shouted and Hazel pulled her feet up behind her. One last leap from Nelson and suddenly they were airborne.

Hazel slammed her eyes shut and grit her teeth to keep from screaming. *Oh my gosh, oh my gosh. We're going to die! Why do women let handsome men talk them into dumb things? Their charming smiles and flattering words have ruled over us for centuries and even now in the age of women's freedom, we still fall for it!*

"Hazel, open your eyes!" Nelson shouted over the wind.

She shook her head.

"I promise it'll be okay. Just open them!"

She heard him laugh and figured if he was laughing, death couldn't be quite as eminent as she feared. Hazel peeled one eye open before the other joined it. She sucked in a gasp. "Oh my heavens..." For someone who made her living with words, Hazel suddenly found herself at a loss for them. The beauty passing below her was indescribable. Green trees in the valley were surrounded by hills filled with grass and wildflowers. Vibrant reds and purples appeared like carpet over the rolling landscape.

"What do you think?" Nelson called back over his shoulder.

"I-I... it's amazing," she answered.

Nelson laughed. "I'd say I've never seen you speechless, but considering how little you talk already, it would be a lie."

Hazel giggled. "Thank you for being patient and not letting me chicken out. This is the best thing ever."

"Woman, you're wounding my ego again! I'm going to have to give you a kiss before you leave that cures you of that comment once and for all."

Hazel felt a zing of excitement shoot up her already overwhelmed nerves. *Why can't he mean that because he likes me, not because he has something to prove?* She shook her head. *Nope. No moping. You are doing something absolutely awe-inspiring. No getting down in the dumps. You can cry your heart out when you get home later tonight.*

"Can you see the water?" Nelson pointed with his head toward a small flash of blue.

"Yeah! Wow! It looks so sparkly from here!"

"Mother Nature must have been in a good mood, because this is absolutely perfect weather. Good wind and sun. Makes for the perfect combo," Nelson said with a smile.

"I'm not usually very fond of the wind, but today... I'll make an exception." Hazel's eyes flew over the horizon, worried she would miss something. It was unreal to be flying over the trees in the open air like this, with full sight of everything down below. Her eyes watered a bit as the wind dried them out, but she didn't even bother to wipe away the tears. *Eh. The wind will dry them anyway.*

NELSON FELT LIKE A proud peacock as he caught glimpses of Hazel's stunned face. Just like when they had repelled down the cliff, she had been frozen solid with fear when they started, but she hadn't run screaming into the hills, she had followed his instructions, trusting him completely.

Her explicit belief that he wouldn't lead her astray was a sensation he'd never had before... and he loved it. Having a reputation as a loafer meant that no one in his family trusted him with anything big. He'd never been tied down and never been in charge, but Hazel saw him differently. She had said so on multiple occasions. She thought he was a good man, a responsible one, a leader, and good with people. She had faith in him and showed it by the fact that she let him bring her on all sorts of daring adventures even though she was scared witless.

Why can't that faith turn into something more? I didn't want to be in a relationship, but I'm falling for this quiet woman and I can't seem to shake it. She's everything I need.

All of the little touches and kisses he'd given her throughout the week had started as a way to protect her from Jack, but had quickly turned into actions he did because he liked it. He liked having her rely on him. He liked having her trust him. He liked pushing her past her boundaries and seeing her expressions when she realized how wonderful life could be.

But she thinks it's all fake, and she isn't interested. She's said exactly that. He sighed.

"You okay over there?" Hazel shouted.

Nelson shook away his depression and smiled back at her. "Yeah. You?"

"Doing great, but you looked like you were trying to solve the mysteries of the universe."

Nelson chuckled. "Nah. Where would be the fun in that? Mystery keeps life interesting."

Hazel laughed and as always, Nelson revelled in the sound. *How am I going to go back to normal life after she's gone?*

Nelson shoved the sad thoughts aside and went back to enjoying the view and Hazel's reactions. It wasn't too long before they were floating over the meadow where his buddy was waiting with the truck.

"Alright, ready to land?" Nelson asked over his shoulder.

"Never!" Hazel laughed. "But I suppose what goes up must come down."

Nelson smiled and nodded. "True stuff, now let's just hope we can get down smoothly."

He felt Hazel stiffen behind him, and he almost laughed out loud. *She's so easy to tease.*

A few minutes later, Nelson's feet hit the ground running as they dropped to the flat, grassy space. His legs pumped and pushed hard to slow down the pace and soon he had the glider rolling on the ground with him, coming to a stop.

His friend, Travis, hustled and began unstrapping them. When Hazel was free, she began jumping around, her hands in the air.

"That was AMAZING!" she shouted. Her wide smile lit up the meadow, and she danced from foot to foot, thoroughly entertaining both men standing watching her.

"I think she enjoyed it," Travis said dryly.

"Really? I hadn't noticed," Nelson responded with a smirk.

"Mission accomplished, Dude. She's putty in your hands." Travis gave him a fist-bump then went back to breaking down the glider.

Nelson felt a small stab in his chest. *I could only wish.*

After everything was taken apart and loaded in Travis's truck, he took Hazel and Nelson back up the hill to their starting point to get Nelson's vehicle. The ride back to the castle was much louder than the ride to the hill. Hazel talked non-stop about everything she had seen and how wonderful it all was.

As they neared the entrance to the resort, Nelson laughed and shook his head. "I had no idea that the way to get you to talk was to take you hang gliding. I'll have to remember that in the future."

Hazel's already red cheeks turned an even deeper shade, and she pinched her lips together. "I'm sorry. I've never done anything quite like that."

Nelson reached over and took her hand, enjoying how soft it was. "Don't be sorry. I'm beyond excited that you enjoyed it and I love hearing you talk. I'd listen to you all day."

Hazel gave him a small self-conscious smile and turned to look out the window, but her hand tightened on his and Nelson took that as a win.

As they pulled into his driveway, Nelson saw another car there and groaned.

"What? What's the matter?" Hazel asked with a frown.

"Put your game face on, Sweetheart. You're about to be smothered."

Hazel's frown deepened. "I don't understand."

"Oh, you will." Nelson sighed and hopped out of the truck.

"Nellie Truman." Ivy stood with her bright red hair floating in the breeze around her and her hands on her hips. The frown on her face was fierce, but her size made her look like a child trying to scold an adult.

"Hey, Fairy Girl," Nelson said cheerfully to his sister-in-law. "What's up?"

"The rumor I heard better not be true," she snapped back.

"And what rumor is that?"

"That you-" Ivy cut off as the other truck door opened.

Nelson hurried over and helped Hazel reach the ground without having to jump.

"Fairy Girl, meet Hazel. Hazel, this is my nutty sister-in-law, Ivy. She's married to Eli." Nelson put his hand to the side of his mouth and fake whispered. "Eli's the *oldest* brother. The bossy one."

Ivy rolled her eyes and closed the distance between her and Hazel with a bright smile. "Hi, Hazel! It's so good to meet you." Her eyes darted over and she glared at Nelson. "Nelson has apparently been hiding you from the family and I came to see him brought to justice."

Nelson dropped his shoulders and tilted his head. "Really? I've been hiding her? We've been on that camp-out all week, Ivy. How exactly was I supposed to introduce you?"

Ivy sniffed and pushed her hair out of her face. "Whatever. You could have mentioned something before you left."

"We didn't start dating until we were on the trip, so..." Nelson raised an eyebrow at the petite woman.

"Fine. I'll give you that. But we still should have a chance to meet her." Ivy turned her bright green eyes back to Hazel's wide, nervous ones. "We're having a family dinner tonight and we'd love to have you join us! Everyone is dying to get to know you. Hayden said you were way too good for this booger," Ivy jerked a thumb in Nelson's direction, "and so we're all curious to figure out why you're with him."

Nelson could see the panic on Hazel's face. "Oh, well, I..." she stammered.

Nelson stepped up and put his arm around Hazel's shoulders, tucking her into his side. "Hazel had been planning to leave for home this afternoon, so I don't know if she can stay."

Ivy's face fell. "Oh. Where do you live?"

Hazel glanced up at Nelson then back over at Ivy. "Just outside of Portland."

Ivy smiled. "Well, that's not too bad. That's what, three hours?"

Hazel nodded. "About that, just a little over."

"You could eat with us and still drive home, or we'd be happy to have you stay at my house for the night and leave first thing in the morning." Ivy chewed her lip. "Is there anything you absolutely have to get back for? Tomorrow's Sunday. Do you have obligations?"

"N-not exactly. I live alone and usually attend church, but that's about it."

Nelson could feel Hazel stiffening in his arms and he squeezed her tighter. He knew Hazel was getting uncomfortable, but he couldn't deny that a few more hours with her would be awesome. He'd been struggling with the idea of letting her go and any delay was welcome.

Hazel's beautiful blue eyes gazed up at him. "What do you want me to do?" she asked quietly.

Nelson couldn't look away. *How has she come to mean so much to me in such a short amount of time? Dang it. This wasn't in the plans.* "Your choice. I won't force you to stay, but my family has great dinners. Hayden usually cooks."

Hazel pinched her lips together, clearly torn. "Umm..." She turned back to Ivy. "I would love to eat dinner with you. Thank you. But I really should head back tonight, even if it is late. I've overstayed my welcome as it is."

"Ah, I doubt someone as sweet as you could do that," Ivy said with a wink and a smile. "Alrighty then, dinner is in just a few hours, so you two get cleaned up from your... what exactly were you doing?" Ivy looked over their windblown state.

"Hang gliding," Nelson said with a grin. "It was Hazel's first time."

"Ah!" Ivy nodded. "Leave it to you to woo a girl by dangling her a hundred feet in the air," Ivy teased. "We'll see you two later. Let's plan on eating at five so we can get done early enough for Hazel to drive safe."

Nelson nodded. "Sounds good."

Nelson kept his arm around Hazel while they watched Ivy get in her car and drive down the graveled trail.

"Are you sure it's okay if I stay to eat? I don't want to cause problems with your family. I mean, they think we're dating and everything." Hazel's eyes were worried as she looked up at him.

Nelson wrapped his other arm around her and squeezed her tight. "It'll be great. You'll get to eat more of Hayden's food and I get to not look like an idiot. It's a win-win." He leaned back and smiled down at her beautiful face. "You going to be okay? My family can be pretty loud and they'll probably rake me over the coals while we're there."

Hazel smiled and shrugged her shoulder. "I have a ton of siblings, remember? I'm used to loud family dinners. Just because I don't add to them doesn't mean I don't know how to handle them."

Nelson couldn't help it. He leaned in and kissed her forehead. "Hazel... you're my favorite," he murmured against her skin. *And I don't know how I'm going to let you go.*

CHAPTER 17

Hazel was sweating and nervous when they pulled into Hayden and Cadence's driveway later that evening. She had showered and dressed in the best clothes she had brought, which was only jeans and a blouse, since she had been packing for a camping trip, but she had done her hair and make-up, hoping she didn't look like a complete outsider.

These people are wealthy and accomplished. I'm just an introverted author who is fake-dating their brother, not to mention falling for him when he's made it clear we're only friends. I definitely don't belong here.

Nelson jumped out of his truck and walked over to where she stood next to her car. "Ready?" he asked with a grin while he grabbed her hand.

"I guess so," she said softly, still staring at the massive log home. Nelson also lived in a mansion, but something about it being Nelson's made it less intimidating. He was so open and friendly, protecting her and taking her under his wing, that his wealthy status didn't bother her as much as it did with the rest of his family.

"You'll be great. And they'll love you," Nelson said, squeezing her hand. "Come on." He led the way up to the door and, without knocking, threw the front door open. "The party is here!" he yelled loudly.

"Do you ever knock?" Hayden yelled from the kitchen, only to have the exotic-looking woman standing next to him whack him across the shoulder. "Ow!" he said, giving the woman a look.

"That's Cadence, Hayden's wife." Nelson said as they walked further into the house and toward the kitchen. Nelson leaned his head toward Hazel's ear, but spoke in a loud whisper. "Cadence can single handedly keep Hayden in line, so don't mess with her. She's scary."

Hayden laughed, only to get another shoulder whack, while Cadence turned her glare to Nelson. "I'm only scary to men who don't seem to be able to grow up." Her gorgeous face turned to Hazel. "However, to more normal people, I'm easy to get along with." Cadence smiled and Hazel had to shake herself out of her stupor. *Oh my word, she's stunning! I'm sinking deeper and deeper here.*

"Hi. Hazel, isn't it?" Cadence raised her eyebrows.

Hazel nodded.

"It's nice to meet you officially. I'm Cadence, this one's," she tilted her head toward Hayden, "keeper and wife." Cadence stuck out her hand.

Hazel tried to swallow and put moisture back in her dry mouth, but it wasn't working very well. "I'm Hazel," she said softly, then mentally slapped herself. *She already knows that!* "Sorry." Hazel scrunched up her face. "Nice to meet you." She tucked into Nelson's side. "I'm a bit nervous."

Cadence chuckled and her low voice was soothing to Hazel's nerves. "No need to be nervous. We all know you've got to be some kind of saint if you stick around with that one." Cadence pointedly looked at Nelson, then back at Hazel. Although it was easy to tell Cadence was teasing, Hazel found herself bothered by the statement.

Nelson was right when he says no one takes him seriously. I might have to correct their assumptions. I mean, it's not like I'll ever see these people after tonight anyway, so who cares if I go out with a bang? Hazel straightened her shoulders and thrust her chin in the air. "Actually, it's Nelson who's been a saint to put up with me. I'm a bit of a scaredy-cat and he took care of me all week."

Cadence paused and an eyebrow rose. Slowly, her gaze turned toward Nelson, who had turned red and was rubbing the back of his neck. She nodded a few times. "That's wonderful to hear. We always wonder how he does on those camping trips and now we have insider information." Cadence smiled and the tension of the moment broke.

Hazel sucked in a long breath. *Score one for Hazel.*

"Where's Eli?" Nelson asked as he led Hazel to the barstools.

"Should be here any minute," Hayden said distractedly over his shoulder. He was currently pulling something out of the oven.

The smell wafted toward Hazel and she nearly groaned in delight. "Oh my word, your husband is the best cook," she said breathlessly to Cadence.

Cadence smiled fondly at Hayden. "Yes he is. And it's a good thing too," her eyes turned to Hazel, "because I'm all thumbs in the kitchen."

Hazel's eyes widened. "Really? You don't cook?"

"If you call burning pancakes and creating charcoal cookies, cooking, then yes, she cooks wonderfully," Hayden said from across the kitchen.

Cadence rolled her eyes and plopped herself onto the stool next to Hazel. "I wish I could say he's wrong, but he's not. I really am terrible." She grinned and shrugged. "Now I have a good excuse for never bringing him breakfast in bed."

Hazel blurted out a laugh then quickly covered her mouth.

Cadence winked. "Don't hide the laugh, it's fine. It's a well-known fact that I'm terrible in the kitchen."

Hazel dropped her hand and let her smile show. "I think it's great that two opposites work together so well."

Cadence studied her for a moment. "Yeah, I guess it's true. Opposites really can be good fits."

Hazel felt heat creeping up her cheeks, knowing Cadence was referring to her and Nelson. *Except ours is fake. So it doesn't matter if opposites attract.*

"Sorry we're late!" Ivy called as they came through the door.

Nelson made an incredulous face at Hayden, then swept his arm toward the newcomers. "How come they don't get in trouble for not knocking?"

Hayden smirked. "Because they're polite about it."

Cadence stood and patted Nelson on the arm. "Don't listen to him, he's just being a jerk."

"Hey! I'm cooking your food here!" Hayden called out.

"Yeah, and you better not burn it," Eli added to the noise.

Hayden turned back to the stove muttering something about unappreciative, uncultured swine.

Hazel's eyes darted around and around, following the quips and conversation that was flowing. *It's just like my family. I miss this.*

"Eli," Eli said, coming toward Hazel with his hand extended.

Hazel took it and gave it a shake. "Hazel," she said softly with a smile. Eli was just as intimidating as Hayden. He wasn't quite as big as the middle brother, but his demeanor was definitely more serious.

"Nice to meet you." His smile softened his face. "I believe you've already met my better half." He reached out an arm for Ivy, tucking her into his side.

"Yes, I did." Hazel replied.

"We're glad to have you here tonight," Ivy said with a wide smile.

"Thank you for the invite. It was very sweet." Hazel clamped her mouth shut at that point, unsure of what else to say. *If I say too much, I might give away that mine and Nelson's relationship isn't real. What would they think then?*

Nelson reached across the barstools and rested his hand on her back. "Yeah well, she's still planning to drive home after dinner, so we need to jump into it. Right, Hayden?" Nelson yelled across the kitchen with a laugh.

"Yeah, yeah. I'm coming," Hayden grumbled. "While the rest of you sit around and chat like a bunch of old ladies."

Ivy laughed, then stepped out of Eli's embrace and into the kitchen. "What can I do to help?"

"Nothing," Hayden said with a grin. "It's time to put things on the table."

"Great. Let's go." Ivy grabbed a dish and walked it over to the table, the rest of the group quickly following her lead.

Once they were seated, Eli led them in grace before they dished up.

"So, Hazel," Eli began as he passed the gratin potatoes, "where are you from again?"

"I, uh, grew up in Vancouver, but now own a home just outside of Portland."

"And how did you and Nelson meet?" Ivy tilted her head and smiled, easing the tension in Hazel's shoulders at the line of questioning.

"Um…" Hazel glanced to Nelson for help.

Nelson read her cue perfectly. "She was on that week long camping trip I just got back from."

"So you just met a few days ago?" Cadence asked.

"Yep," Nelson said with a grin.

"But I thought Hayden said you two were dating?" Cadence frowned.

"We are." Nelson's eyebrows shot up. "Not all of us fight for a year before admitting we like someone."

"Watch it," Hayden growled.

"Sorry," Cadence said with a smile. "It's fine, just surprised me."

Hayden retorted. "I'm not sure why. It would make total sense for him to jump into something."

Hazel felt her cheeks warm again. *Why can't they say something nice about him?* Taking a deep breath, she burst out, "Is there really any kind of timeline on two people who enjoy each other's company? Nelson was the perfect gentleman and protector this week and there was really no way I could keep from falling for him." She stuffed a bite of chicken in her mouth to stop from saying more.

The entire table stopped what they were doing to look at her and Hazel felt every individual eyeball. *Now you've done it.* She ducked her head and refused to make eye contact with anyone.

After a strained moment of silence, Nelson reached over and covered her closed fist with his warm hand. Her eyes darted up to his, and she lost her breath. His gaze was warm and looked completely besotted. *Why does this have to be an act?* Her heart pinched.

"Well, Nellie," Ivy said with a grin. "It's clear you did alright this week." Ivy's eyes darted back and forth between Hazel and Nelson, happiness lighting her features.

"You have no idea," Nelson murmured, picking up Hazel's hand and kissing the back of it.

Oh my word, could he be any more perfect?

NELSON WATCHED THE pink deepen on Hazel's cheeks and had to fight the desire to kiss that spot as well, rather than just her hand, but he knew she was embarrassed enough as it was. He had never had anyone stand up for him against his family before and for it to be the quiet girl he had fallen for made it even more momentous.

Hazel finally broke their staring contest and cleared her throat. "Why do you call him Nellie?" she asked Ivy.

Ivy grinned and pumped her eyebrows. "He's called me Fairy Girl since I came to work at the resort, so I gave him a nickname back: Nellie." She shrugged. "He hated it, so it was perfect."

Hazel gave a small smile and nodded, then picked up her fork and started to eat again.

"She's like a kid sister to me, so I let her get away with it where others would get a pounding," Nelson whispered in her ear.

Hazel made a choking noise and covered her mouth as she laughed. After she had swallowed, she turned to him. "So you're saying I can't call you Nellie?"

I shouldn't. I really shouldn't. But how can I turn down such an opportunity? Nelson let his eyes smolder with his true feelings as he looked at her and leaned in until they were nose to nose. Hazel's eyes widened and he could hear her breathing change. "You… have permission to call me anything you want," he said in a husky voice. He waited a moment longer, drawing out the tension in the room. "As long as it starts with 'man of' and ends with, 'my dreams.'"

Her lips twitched and her eyes crinkled before Hazel burst out laughing. Nelson joined in and wrapped an arm around her shoulders, pulling her in so he could kiss the side of her head. Once he let her go and their laughter died down, he realized the table was once again silent.

Looking up, Nelson was surprised to once again see every eye turned to them. Both of his brothers appeared to be in shock, while the women were studying he and Hazel like they were bugs in a laboratory. *Time for a subject change.*

"Speaking of kid sisters, when are Laken and Teagan arriving?" Nelson shoved a bite of roll into his mouth and looked around in expectation.

Eli cleared his throat and shook his head. "A couple of weeks. Teagan had some loose ends to tie up at the nursery she's been working at."

Nelson nodded, his mouth still full.

"Oh? What does she do with plants?" Hazel asked politely.

"She just graduated as a botanist," Ivy explained. "Her twin sister, Laken, graduated as an aesthetician. They're moving to the resort to join their brothers and to open branches of their own on the property."

"Oh." Hazel nodded, but it was easy to see she was still a little confused.

"We're having a greenhouse built for Teagan," Cadence jumped in. "She's going to grow fresh produce for Hayden year round, but it will also give her a chance to do her own studies and experiments."

"That's neat," Hazel said with a smile.

"Yeah, but I have to admit I'm looking forward to Laken's side of things. We're having a spa built for her, which she will be the director of," Ivy piped back in. She sighed and closed her eyes. "I've only ever had a facial and massage on my honeymoon and I intend to try out every service she's going to offer."

"Sounds good to me!" Cadence added.

"You should come up when it's open and join us for a girls' weekend!" Ivy said excitedly.

"That would be fantastic," Cadence added with a nod, also looking at Hazel.

Nelson looked down to see what Hazel thought of their invitation.

She had shrunk into herself a little and a polite smile was on her face. "We'll have to see," she murmured, avoiding any kind of commitment.

I knew it. I knew it! So why does it hurt every time she reminds me that this isn't going to last? Nelson focused on his food in order to keep the disappointment from showing on his face.

The conversation picked up and soon dinner and dessert were things of the past.

They had all been laughing at a story Hayden had been telling when Hazel put her hand on Nelson's forearm, drawing his attention.

"Nelson, I really should head out so I don't get in too late," she said softly.

Nelson glanced at the wall clock. "Oh yeah, I hadn't realized how long we'd been talking." He scooted back his seat. "Hazel is ready to go, so I'm going to walk her out," he announced as he pulled out her chair.

"Let me just run these dishes to the sink first," she murmured.

"Oh, no! Don't you worry about those," Cadence said with a smile. "We've got plenty of help for dishes. You just go say goodbye to Nelson."

Hazel paused as if uncertain, then nodded her gratitude. "Alright, thank you so much for your hospitality. Dinner was delicious, Hayden."

Hayden beamed. "Thanks, I'm glad you enjoyed it. And it was a pleasure to meet you."

"You too." Hazel smiled and turned to follow Nelson to the door.

"Oh, you're not getting away that easy!" Ivy said as she jumped up from her seat. She rounded the table and grabbed Hazel in a bear hug.

Hazel was stiff for a moment before wrapping her arms around Ivy and hugging her back. He frowned when he saw Ivy whisper something in Hazel's ear. She leaned back and looked at the redhead for a moment before nodding.

"That's all I needed to know," Ivy said. "Alright, Nellie, she's all yours," Ivy said with a wink.

"I would come hug you too," Cadence called from her seat, "but I try not to assault people until they're comfortable around me."

Ivy gasped and put her hands to her chest in mock outrage. "That wasn't nice." She sniffed and put her nose in the air. "Assaulting people helps them get to know you better."

Chuckles floated around the room and Hazel's smile was genuine as she looked at Nelson.

"Ready?" he asked softly.

She nodded.

Nelson reached out, grabbed her hand, and took off for the door, ignoring the jokes being vaulted his way from his brothers.

Once outside, he closed the door and took a deep breath. "Sorry about them. I'm usually the one doing the teasing, so it was odd tonight to be on the other side of it." He scrunched up his face and ran his hand through his hair.

Hazel gave a light laugh. "Probably good for you to see how the rest of us live," she teased.

Nelson used the hand he was holding to pull her in close. Her light floral scent hit his nose, and he nearly groaned. *Shoot. How am I going to do this? She's made it clear she only thinks of me as a friend, that she's not right for me.* His gaze locked on her lips. He wanted desperately to kiss her until she couldn't breathe. To hold her until she melted in his arms. To throw her over his shoulder and lock her away until she promised to love him back.

Nelson's eyes widened as his thoughts screeched to a halt. *No way... that can't be right. I'm not in love with her? Am I?*

Frustrated that he didn't seem to know his own mind, Nelson forced the thoughts aside. *Just say goodbye. You've got to say goodbye right now, don't worry about anything else.*

Hazel was looking up at him with a concerned expression. "Nelson, is everything all right?"

He cleared his throat and took a step back, letting go of her hand. "Yeah. Yeah. Everything is fine."

Her shoulders seemed to droop as he distanced himself, but Nelson could already feel his heart hurting, knowing she was leaving and never coming back.

"Okay... well, thank you," she said softly. "This was probably one of the best weeks I've ever had." She smiled at him and Nelson had to fist his hands to keep from reaching out.

"Yeah, it was fun. Thanks for playing along with everything, especially after we got back. My family loved you." He looked at the ground and dug his toe into the dirt.

"Well, thank you for helping to protect me in the first place. I've never had someone stand up for me like that before. And your patience in getting me through all of our adventures was amazing." Hazel shook her head and gave a self-deprecating smile. "*You* are amazing!" She walked up to him and put a hand on his chest. Nelson's nerves came alive and his eyes shot to hers. "I know you think you're the black sheep of the family, but I can tell your family loves you, even if they do make teasing comments sometimes. And regardless of what they think, you need to know that you'll always be my hero."

Slowly she leaned in and Nelson held his breath. His hand slid to her hips, lightly touching as he waited to see if she would kiss him. *Come on, Haze. Give me a sign. Let me know you like me too. Please...*

Disappointment felt like a sledgehammer as she turned her trajectory at the last minute and gave him a light kiss on the cheek.

"Thank you, Nelson. I'll never forget you," she said softly, then turned and walked to her car.

Nelson's tongue was just as numb as the rest of him. After she climbed in her car and the headlights came on, Nelson gave her a small wave as she pulled out and drove into the night.

He rubbed his sternum as an ache settled into his chest. *It's true. I do love her. The first girl to stand up for me and think I'm worth something and I fell in love with her... but she doesn't love me back.*

Nelson glanced over his shoulder at the house where his family was waiting and knew he couldn't face them. Not a single part of him wanted to go back inside and have them ask questions and rehash everything that had happened this week.

Shaking his head and stuffing his hands in his pockets, he took off down the road, not even bothering to collect his keys from inside.

CHAPTER 18

Sunlight streamed in through Hazel's windows, waking her from a dead slumber. It had taken her almost the whole night to calm down enough to sleep. Driving home in the dark when your heart was breaking had proved not to be the smartest move she had ever made.

Her eyes were puffy and gritty from hours of crying in the car and in her bed. Soothing chamomile tea, lavender in the diffuser- she had tried everything last night, but nothing had taken her mind off the fact that her heart had been left up at Avangarde Castle.

Groaning, she rolled over and threw her arm over her face. "Ow," she muttered, when she whacked her nose. "How could I be such an idiot? Why in the world didn't I just stop that stupid fake relationship to begin with? If he hadn't been so sweet and so wonderful, then I wouldn't be in this mess!"

Liar, her inner voice cried. Nelson was the perfect guy for her because of who he was, not because he had been pretending to be her boyfriend. She thought of how he had protected her from Jack's unwanted advances. She thought of how he had spoken so soothingly to her when she'd been frightened out of her wits. She thought of how he had celebrated with her when she'd overcome her fears enough to try whatever activity they were doing. She thought of his sweet kisses and him sitting in her tent eating dinner in the rain. She thought of his warm hand on hers and his mischievous grin.

A frown pulled at her lips and she sniffled again. "Ugh!" she cried, sitting up in bed and wiping more tears from her cheeks. "This is ridiculous! I knew from the start he didn't like me that way, but I didn't listen. I just fell for him anyway. He made it clear it wasn't real, that it was all for show so that Jack would leave me alone. And I had to go and ruin that."

Her scolding didn't matter. Her heart still felt like it had been shredded and her tears continued to stream unheeded down her cheeks. With a defeated sigh, she plopped back down on the bed. "Maybe... maybe I'll allow myself a day to cry. Just twenty-four hours of a major pity party and then I have to move on. I have to get up and live my life, because no matter how wonderful he is, he's not mine and sitting here pining for him won't do anybody any good." She wiped at her eyes again. "Besides, I have a book to write."

With a firm nod at her plan, Hazel curled up under the covers and squeezed her eyes shut. *Just twenty-four hours. So enjoy it while you can.*

True to her word, Hazel allowed herself to fall apart for one day. The morning after her breakdown, she got up and forced herself to shower and eat breakfast. With her hair wadded up in a wet knot on top of her head and a steaming cup of mint tea in her hands, she sat down at her small breakfast table.

To her right she had a stack of notebooks full of scribblings from her week at Avangarde. In front of her was her open laptop with a blank page staring at her and to her left she set her tea.

"Right," she said with a nod. "Time to get this show on the road. If I can't have Nelson myself, then by golly, I will write him with the right person. He deserves a happy ever after."

Putting her hands on the keyboard, she took off. Feverishly typing the story of her week, with one significant change. Instead of a mousy, quiet girl joining Nelson on his trip, he had a strong, confident, beautiful woman as his companion.

One who wasn't afraid of repelling off a mountain. One who knew how to set up and take down her own tent. One who stood toe to toe with Jack and put him in his place. Instead of being protected by nineteen-year-old girls, Hazel's main character was the envy of other women.

"She's everything Nelson needs," she muttered as she wrote.

For two weeks, Hazel pounded out the story. By the time she had typed 'The End', her fingers were nearly in a permanent cramped position. With a smile, Hazel leaned back from her computer screen.

"Oh, man," she groaned. "I have sat here too long!" Standing up, she began to stretch her back and work her fingers. "Good thing that story was worth it," she muttered as she manually moved her aching fingers.

"Time to celebrate." Heading to the kitchen, Hazel dug around in her freezer until she found her favorite ice cream, then grabbed a spoon. Leaning against the countertop, gazing out into her tiny backyard, Hazel watched the leaves and branches of her trees ripple in the breeze. A bird hopped along one of the lower branches, reminding Hazel of what it had felt like to fly through the air when Nelson had taken her hang gliding.

The familiar sting of tears stung her eyes, and she blinked hard, pulling her eyes away from the sight. "You just gave him the perfect happy ever after," she scolded. "No feeling sorry for yourself that you weren't that person."

Her mind wandered to the story she had just finished. *People are going to love it,* she thought. But a tiny worry niggled at the back of her mind. Hazel frowned. "What's there to worry about?" she muttered around a mouthful of ice cream. She shook her head and put the ice cream away.

"There's nothing to worry about. This is exactly how this story should have gone." Hazel glanced at the clock on the wall. "Ooh, if I hurry I can make that Zumba class at the rec tonight."

Hurrying up the stairs, Hazel ignored the little thoughts of doubt and got dressed to go sweat.

But two days later, the doubts had turned into full-blown anxiety. Hazel couldn't sleep and her heart nagged at her that her story wasn't right.

Letting out a growl, Hazel climbed from her bed in the early morning hours and stomped to the kitchen table. Opening her laptop, she glared at the brightly glowing screen.

"What do you want?" she said in a tired voice. "I wrote the story. It's great. Probably one of my best. What do you want?"

The cursor blinked at her, nonplussed at the frustration in her tone.

It wasn't right. That's not the story your heart really wants to tell.

Rubbing her hands down her face, Hazel growled at the words from her inner voice. "I already wrote it! Why can't you just be happy with that?"

It's not the right story.

Hazel threw up her hands. "The real story isn't what people want to read," she whined, laying her head on the table. "The real story is about a girl who's a chicken. A girl who couldn't 'fess up to her feelings. A girl who was more a burden than a friend to the guy she fell in love with. I need a story that will sell copies. I mean, even an author has to pay the bills! Nobody wants to read about scaredy-cats who don't get their man."

Not good enough. Nelson obviously enjoyed your company. He asked you to stay an extra day and took you on an adventure. He introduced you to his family. He showed you what it was like to fly.

Hazel's mind went back to when she had eaten dinner with the Trumans. Cadence's words about opposites attracting seem to ring through her ears while Ivy's private question about Hazel's feeling solidified the answer.

"Okay... I might not have gotten him in real life, but maybe I can write the real story with the ending it should have had." She scrunched her nose and wiggled her fingers over the keyboard. "Could Nelson and I have worked out if I'd been more brave?"

The possibilities began to ruminate in her head and she couldn't stop the momentum.

This. This is what you should write. Tell about how you fell in love with your fake billionaire boyfriend.

Those dang tears pricked at her eyes again, but Hazel bit the inside of her cheek, refusing to let them fall. "Okay... okay..." she said softly. "Let's try this again."

POPPYCOCK STOMPED HIS hoof as Nelson brushed the horse's rump. "Sorry, old boy, didn't mean to brush too hard," Nelson grumbled before easing up on his hurried movements.

The horse turned his head and pushed Nelson's shoulder. "Yeah... I know... I know." Nelson scratched the horse's forehead, then pushed him away.

Finishing his work, Nelson stepped back and dropped the brush into his work bucket with a clang.

"Hey, Boss," Daniel said with a grin, resting his arms over the stall door.

"Hey, Man. What's up?"

"The guys and I are done putting everything away. Just wondering if you had more for us to do?"

"Nah." Nelson took off his hat and scratched his head before slipping it back on. "Go on and go home. You guys deserve the rest."

"Thanks, Boss Man!" Daniel grinned and saluted Nelson before walking toward the front of the barn.

Nelson grabbed the bucket of supplies and headed out of the stall. Once the bucket was put away, Nelson took a final walk through the barn to check on everything.

"I think it's about time you headed home too," a gruff voice called out from behind him. "Isn't that supposed to be one of the privileges of being the boss?"

Nelson forced a grin and turned around to talk to Tom, his head employee. "Hey, Tom. I think we got it all done for the night."

Tom nodded slowly, eyeing Nelson. "Yes. And every other night since you got back from that long camping trip."

Nelson clenched his jaw to keep from reacting to the comment. He knew he hadn't been himself lately. *I mean, geez. How can someone be normal when their heart drove away almost a month ago?*

Tom put his hands on his hips and tilted his head. "You ever gonna tell me what happened that week?"

Nelson shrugged. "Nothing to tell."

Tom shook his head. "Mr. Truman, I wasn't born yesterday. Now, you don't have to tell me anything. In fact, my wife would tell you I'm a terrible listener, but it's plain as day that something happened. And it's even clearer that what happened involved a woman."

Nelson scowled. "Where did you get that idea?"

"Age and experience." Tom turned and headed back toward his office space. "I'd be happy to work on my listening skills if you want, or you could find someone who would be a mite more help than this old cowboy."

Nelson watched him go. His hands clenched and unclenched as he fought the frustration inside of him. *Would talking to someone help? Then who? I like Tom, but I don't really want to spill all my secrets to him.*

With a sigh of defeat, Nelson turned and walked to a side door. Leaving the barn, he climbed into his truck and headed for home. For the past month, he had been staying late at the castle avoiding his cabin like the plague.

He used to love being home. He entertained people all day long and at home, he could put his feet up and relax. No one to tease, no one to crack a joke for, no media camera to smile for. But now... his home felt empty. Large, empty and quiet. Hazel had barely spent any time inside his cabin, but it had been enough for Nelson to get a good picture of her in his head.

He could still see her walking around, her bright, blue eyes wide with wonder and awe. He could even smell the light, flowery scent that followed her wherever she went. It made him want to pull her in close, run his fingers through that soft, blonde hair and kiss her perfect lips.

He had become desperate after a week and had looked her up online. Her author profile on Facebook was easy to find, but her private one was locked down tight. He had debated over and over about sending a friend request, but the way she left things the night after dinner kept stopping him. Trying to get glimpses of her by following her author page had proved fruitless as she only posted about sales or funny reading memes.

"Aargh!" he yelled, slamming his hand on his steering wheel. "This is so stupid! We barely knew each other! Not to mention I have no plans to settle down. This is supposed to be my time to shine! My time to look good in the media!"

He slumped and slowed down the truck as he pulled into his garage. "Then why does it feel like those dreams are the stupid ones?"

He walked inside and stormed into his bedroom. Putting on his swim trunks, Nelson headed to his backyard and pulled the top off his hot tub. He turned on the jets and settled in, resting his head on the edge and closing his eyes.

"Don't fall asleep," a feminine voice called out to him

Nelson jerked upright, splashing water over the sides. "Ivy? Is that you?" He narrowed his eyes and stared into the darkness. Nelson hadn't bothered to turn on the lights he had around the jacuzzi and it was difficult to see more than a couple feet from him.

"Yep!" A metal sound screeched through the air as she dragged one of Nelson's patio chairs over next to where he sat.

Nelson huffed and settled back in, resting his head and eyes. "I'm not really in an entertaining mood tonight, Fairy Girl. And besides, isn't that my brother's job now?"

Ivy barked a laugh. "Your brother is in Seattle for the night. Some business meeting or something."

Nelson cracked an eye open. "Why didn't you go with him?"

Ivy glared at him. "None of your business."

He raised an eyebrow. "You come here, infiltrate my home without my permission, and say it's none of my business?"

She sniffed and put her nose in the air. "I didn't infiltrate your home. I'm not even in your home."

"Whatever," Nelson mumbled and closed his eye again. "But I was serious when I said I wasn't good company tonight."

"Nellie, you haven't been good company since Hazel left."

Nelson winced at her name. *Why does that hurt so much? Stupid heart.*

Silence reigned for a moment and Nelson opened his eyes to see what Ivy was doing. She had settled herself into the chair she brought over and was looking at him with a sympathetic expression on her face.

"Spill it," she said softly.

Nelson opened his mouth to ask, 'spill what?', but snapped it shut again. *Ivy is probably the perfect person to talk to about it. Maybe it'll help, like Tom said.* "It wasn't real," he whispered hoarsely.

Ivy leaned her head forward. "What? What wasn't real?"

Nelson sat up and shook the water from his hair. "Hazel. Our relationship. None of it was real."

Ivy blinked several times and frowned. "I think I need you to explain that a little more."

"I faked being her boyfriend to keep that Jack dude from hitting on her," he said through gritted teeth. "Man... it's all so... STUPID!" he yelled, slapping a hand in the water.

Ivy's eyes widened, and she jerked back a little. "Um... Nellie, I think you need to calm down."

He rubbed his hands down his face. "Yeah, I know. Sorry."

"Why don't you start from the beginning, huh? Tell me everything."

Nelson nodded and folded his arms over his chest. "Yeah. Alright." Over the next half hour Nelson poured out everything. From meeting

Hazel in the castle hallways and thinking she was cute to realizing she was the girl who left without eating because Jack had tried to come onto her.

He talked about helping her when she got scared and how the two teenage girls ended up being his biggest cheerleaders. He talked about how Hazel had the most beautiful blue eyes and how she made him feel ten feet tall. How she thought he was worth something when nobody else seemed to think so. And finally, how he now felt lonely and miserable without her.

Ivy rubbed her temple. "I don't get it. Why don't you just call her? I mean, it can't be that hard. You like her, so keep in touch. Try to see her again. She's only a couple hours away. You with your big billionaire lifestyle, you can make that work easily."

"I thought of that," Nelson spit out, then took a deep breath. "Sorry. I thought of trying to stay in touch, but it just seemed too painful, especially after she made it so clear that we weren't compatible for each other. It started out fake to her and ended that way." He frowned. "I'm the only one it changed for."

Ivy chewed her lip for a moment. "I'm not sure I believe that. I mean, at that family dinner, she looked at you like you hung the moon. Women don't just look at anybody like that."

"That's just Hazel. She was always telling me how great I was." He stared into the black forested area around his home. "She didn't like me feeling like I was the black sheep of the family."

"The black sheep-" Ivy rolled her eyes. "Nellie, no one thinks you're the black sheep of the family. If we had a black sheep, it would probably be Laken, not you."

Nelson snorted. "Being spoiled doesn't make her the black sheep. I'm the one who everyone thinks is just a mooch. I'm the one who didn't finish college. I mean, how often do Eli and Hayden talk about how all I do is play all day?"

"Nellie..." she chided. "They're your brothers. You tease them to high heaven, so... they tease back. Now Hayden, well, he might do it with a little more bite, but they still love you. And besides, Hayden bites at everybody."

"Tell him to save it for his food," Nelson grumbled.

Ivy laughed and wiped a stray hair out of her face. "But anyway, back to my point. I think Hazel has real feelings for you, but you said yourself how quiet and shy she is. She probably didn't have the courage to say it out loud. When she left from dinner, I asked her if she was falling for you and she said yes. You don't think she just flat out lied to me, do you?"

Nelson snorted. "Why not? The whole thing was a lie. Not to mention, she had every opportunity when we were saying goodbye to say something. If she had just shown me a little," he pinched two fingers together, "sign, I would have jumped on the opportunity. But she kissed me on the cheek. On the cheek! Like a stinkin' brother!"

"Nelson Truman. You're being ridiculous. Why didn't you just kiss her? Let her know *your* feelings have changed? Why did it have to be Hazel who said something?"

"I guess because I had been the one initiating things all week. I always took her hand. I always kissed her. I put my arm around her. It was always me. I thought she would get it. Get that I liked putting my arm around her. Liked holding her hand. Liked kissing her," he grumbled.

"You really do have it bad, don't you? I've never heard you talk so seriously before." Ivy's lips turned downward.

Nelson just grunted and folded his arms.

"I really think you should call her, Nelson. I understand why you want her to make the first move, but sometimes you just have to take life by the horns. Isn't giving up your pride worth possibly getting her back?"

Nelson scowled. "Who asked you to be all logical here? I thought when you had girlie talk it was supposed to be all emotional and stuff. You're supposed to sympathize with me."

Ivy laughed and stood. "I do. Feeling like someone doesn't return your feelings sucks. I know."

Nelson nodded. Ivy did know. Her relationship with Eli had been rough for a while.

"But I already told you I think she likes you. Which is what anyone would want to hear. You just don't believe me, so I had to dig out my rational side." She picked up the chair she had been sitting in and put it back where it belonged.

"Whatever."

Ivy shrugged. "Clearly you don't want to hear what I have to say. But I think you should go after her."

Nelson grunted again.

"Alright, well, I'll leave you to your sulking, but you have my opinion and you know where to find me if you want to talk again." Ivy started to walk toward the side of the house.

"You never did say why you came over or why you didn't go with Eli," Nelson hollered at her.

Ivy walked back to the light. "I came because I had the time and I've been worried about you. I stayed because my morning sickness makes road trips horrible right now."

Nelson froze. "W-what? Morning sickness?"

Ivy grinned. "Yep!" She turned and headed back out. "See ya later, Uncle Nellie!" she called over her shoulder.

A slow smile crossed over Nelson's face. "You better not teach them to call me Nellie!" he finally shouted after her.

Ivy's laughter could be heard floating through the air.

"Uncle Nellie. Holy cow..." He whistled under his breath. "Now if only we could get there to be an Aunt Hazel," he lamented.

He pulled himself out of the water and sat on the edge of the hot tub, letting the night air cool him from sitting so long in the hot water.

Putting his elbows on his knees, he rested his chin in his hands and let his mind wander to what Ivy had said. "Was she telling Ivy the truth? Should I have said something? Would she be willing to entertain the idea of us being together?" He squeezed his eyes shut. "If she said no, would it really be any worse than it is now?"

His thoughts swirled in a chaotic pattern and he couldn't seem to get them to stop. "Ahh... I can't think straight." He climbed out of the tub and grabbed a towel out of the supply closet. While drying himself, his stomach rumbled, and he grimaced. "Dinner and bed. I'll think on it again in the morning."

CHAPTER 19

Several more mornings came and went and Nelson was no closer to making a move than he had been when he and Ivy talked.

Every time he talked himself into going down to see her, he'd freeze up. Fear that she would laugh at him or reject him kept Nelson from ever taking that first step.

"Why is it that the guy who isn't afraid to jump off cliffs is terrified of speaking to a woman?" he muttered while hosing the cobwebs off one of his kayaks. "I can leap without looking, but facing down the shy, quiet woman I love has me cowering like a baby." He growled, frustrated at himself, but still unable to do anything about it.

He was so caught up in his own thoughts that he didn't hear Ivy approach him from behind.

"Nellie!" she shouted, slapping him on the shoulder.

"What the-" Nelson whirled around, the hose shooting in front of him and smacking Eli straight in the chest. "Dude!" Nelson turned the water away and quickly walked to the spigot to turn it off. "Sorry, Eli! I didn't see you there." Nelson pinched his lips between his teeth, but it didn't help. He bent over as he howled at Eli's soaked clothes and angry face.

Ivy stood next to her husband laughing just as hard as Nelson.

Eli peeled his wet polo away from his chest with a look of disgust on his face. "I'm thrilled I could be your amusement today," he said drily.

"Sorry, Hon. But you have to admit that was pretty awesome." Ivy sighed and wiped her eyes as her laughter calmed down.

"For you, maybe," Eli grumbled, flapping his shirt back and forth to dry it off.

"Sorry," Nelson sputtered again. "I really didn't mean to spray you."

Eli raised an eyebrow. "When you least expect it, Punk... when you least expect it."

Ivy frowned and smacked the back of her hand on Eli's arm. "Alright, Big Talker. That's enough of that."

"So what brought the two soon-to-be parents to my humble abode?" Nelson asked.

Eli's eyes immediately softened at Nelson's words and he turned to his tiny wife with a smile.

"No, please..." Nelson closed his eyes and groaned. His heart pinched as he saw the obvious love the two had for each other. *Why couldn't Hazel and I look like that?* "I really can't take any more of the gushy stuff, not today."

"Sorry," Ivy said softly. "But we did come by for a reason. I found something I think you should have."

Nelson raised an eyebrow. "And what is that?"

"A book."

"A book," Nelson said bluntly. "You want me to have a book?"

Ivy bit her lip and nodded excitedly. "Yes. But this isn't just any book."

Nelson gave her a deadpan look. "What is it, Fairy Girl?"

Ivy brought the book out from behind her back and held it out.

Nelson took it and read the title. "Falling for the Billionaire"; An Opposites Attract, romantic comedy." Nelson scrunched up his face and glanced at Ivy's beaming face. Looking back down, he caught his breath. "By Hazel Thurgood," he choked out. "What is this?"

"It's her latest book," Eli said with a grin. "Just released a few days ago."

"H-how did you know about it?"

Ivy's smug grin was still plastered on her face when she shrugged and stuck her nose in the air. "I've been following her online ever since dinner when she mentioned she was an author. So, I knew when it came out and I ordered it immediately."

Nelson just kept his eyes glued to the small paperback.

"Read the back," Ivy encouraged.

Turning it over, Nelson read the story premise and his jaw dropped. "She did it. She wrote a story about us."

"Yes!" Ivy squealed. "Only I don't think it's quite how she said it would be."

Nelson raised a questioning brow. "What do you mean?"

"Read it and find out," Ivy said with a pump of her eyebrows. "Come on, Sweetheart, I need food." Ivy grabbed Eli's hand, and he quickly began walking her back to their car.

"Read it!" Eli shouted over his shoulder.

"Yeah. Got it..." Nelson said distractedly as he continued to stare at the book. *This is the one. The one she said she might write, but would replace herself with someone bolder and less shy.* He frowned. "But that means it wouldn't be an opposites attract if that was the case."

He stumbled over to a bench and opened up to the first page. For the next couple of hours, Nelson ignored everything except the story. And when he finally read the last paragraph, a wide smile sat on his face.

He sat for a couple more breaths before jumping from the bench and hurrying inside. He grabbed his cell as he began throwing clothes into a duffle bag.

"Ivy!" he shouted when she finally picked up. "I need her address!"

"Hmm... what will you give me for it?" she teased.

"Not a good time," he growled, pinching the phone between his shoulder and chin while he zipped up the bag.

Ivy laughed. "We'll just say you owe me, okay?"

"Fine. Where is she?"

Ivy rattled off the address she had found and Nelson punched it into his GPS app. "Thanks! I'll be gone for a few days."

"Have fun!" Ivy called out right before he ended the call.

HAZEL SIGHED AND SMILED when she checked her rankings for the tenth time that day. "Falling for the Billionaire" was proving to be one of the best decisions she had ever made. Within only a couple days of its release, it had taken off and was still soaring.

She had made it to the top of a couple of best-seller lists online and was having a great time watching her book thrive.

"Now if only the author could do the same," she said softly, her smile fading.

Reliving her time with Nelson had been difficult. During the first draft of the book, it had been easier because she had filled someone else in for herself. But writing it as herself was harder. She had poured her heart into every word. Every emotion and sensation that had occurred during her week with Nelson Truman was written for all to see. *And that's why people like it. It's real,* that dang inner voice reminded her.

"Yeah, I got it," she grumbled back.

As much as she was enjoying her success, it felt empty to not have anyone to share it with. She wasn't someone who dated often, so she was used to being alone. Especially since she was an introvert. But having a fake boyfriend for a few days had changed something inside of her and she found herself wishing she could share her exciting success with another person.

Not just a person. Nelson. You want to share it with Nelson.

A tear slowly trickled down her cheek and Hazel wiped it away. "Yeah. I want to share it with Nelson," she admitted with a shake of her head. "When am I ever going to get over him?" But even as she asked the question, she knew the answer.

Never. We never truly forget our first love.

Hazel had finally had to admit that she was completely in love with Nelson as she wrote their story. Her emotions were too real and too raw to be anything but love.

"And you never even told him," she scolded. That was the only thing she had changed about the book. At the very end, instead of her chickening out and kissing Nelson's cheek, Hazel had given her character the courage to kiss him dead on the lips and whisper how she felt about him.

Of course, the hero had returned her feelings, and they had had an epic happy ever after. "One for the books," Hazel said through a watery chuckle.

Bang, bang, bang.

"What?" Hazel jerked up and put her hand to her pounding heart. "Good grief, who the heck is that?" She quickly wiped the lingering tears on her cheeks and glanced in the mirror next to the door before pulling it open.

"Oh my gosh." Her knees buckled and Hazel gripped the side of the door to stay upright. "Nelson..." she breathed.

"Hazel," he said just as tenderly. His hair was wild and looked like he had been running his hands through it over and over again. There was a couple of day's worth of stubble on his face and dark circles under his eyes. Eyes that seemed to devour her as they looked her over from head to toe.

"W-what are you-" Hazel's eyes widened, and she nearly fell again when she saw the paperback in his hand. "My book..."

Nelson's eyes drifted down to his hand then back to her. "Did you mean it?"

"Did I mean what?" Hazel's heart rate skyrocketed, and it suddenly grew difficult to breathe.

"The ending. Did you mean it?"

Paralyzing fear hit Hazel straight in the chest and took control of her air supply. She couldn't breathe and she couldn't seem to talk. *Do*

I tell him? Do I tell him that that's how I wish it had gone? That I'll be forever sorry that I was too scared to say anything? How many people get a second chance like this? But am I brave enough to take it?

"I-I," she forced words out of her mouth, but couldn't get anything to make sense.

The light in Nelson's eyes began to dim, and he leaned back a little.

No! Hazel screamed at herself. He came all the way here. Say something! "Yes," she finally whispered.

Nelson's eyebrows shot up.

Hazel cleared her throat and tried again. "Yes, I meant it." She took a shuddering breath, and she felt her eyes tear up. "I wish I had had the courage to tell you before, but I-" she gave a self-deprecating laugh, "I'm such a wuss. I completely fell in love wi-"

Hazel's confession was cut off as Nelson dropped the book and swooped in to kiss her. His arms wrapped around her back and pulled her into his chest. His touch banished the fear that had been holding her back and her nerves began to sing at their exchange.

Throwing her arms around his neck, she raised herself up on tiptoe in order to get closer to him.

Nelson chuckled through their kiss, then slid one of his hands into her hair, deepening the kiss.

I've died and gone to heaven. Oh my gosh, how can any of this be real? Her fingers played with his hair and she snuggled in even closer.

Nelson let go of her lips and started plying her face with kisses. "Hazel," he said between pecks. "How could we have been so stupid?"

"Mmm... what?" she asked with her eyes still closed. Her mind had turned to mush several minutes ago and wasn't willing to concentrate just yet.

Nelson chuckled again. "How about we go inside and talk? I'm pretty sure your neighbors are watching the show we're making."

Hazel blinked and snapped out of her daze. "Oh heavens. Yeah, let's get inside." Hazel grabbed his hand and closed the door behind them before leading him to the couch.

Nelson sat then promptly pulled Hazel into his lap.

"Oh!" she squeaked before grinning and giving him a short kiss. "How did you get here?"

Nelson wrapped his arms around her waist and tucked her into his chest before talking. "I hate to say it, but I have to give credit to the fairy girl."

Hazel turned her face up. "Ivy?"

"Yeah..." He sighed and ran a hand through his hair. "Before I confess everything, I just want to double check." He cleared his throat. "You love me, right?"

Hazel nodded solemnly. "Do you-"

"Yes. Absolutely," Nelson said with a grin. "Sorry. I was too busy to say it back on the front porch."

Hazel felt her blush creep up her cheeks even as she smiled in joy.

Nelson groaned and ran a finger over her cheek. "That blush kills me," he said softly. "But I gotta get this out first, then we can get back to making up for lost time."

Hazel laughed lightly and settled back in.

For the next hour they kissed, laughed, and swapped confessions about their time together during the camping trip.

Hazel buried her forehead in the crook of his neck as she groaned. "I can't believe I didn't see it! You kept bringing up the fact that our relationship wasn't real and I thought it was because you didn't want me to get any ideas about making it real."

Nelson squeezed her even closer. "You were always so quiet, I thought it was because you were uncomfortable with the thought of us being real. So, I kept saying it to reassure you that you were safe."

"You were right, we have been so stupid. Instead of moping around eating ice cream every night, I could have been talking to you, texting with you-"

"Kissing me," Nelson interrupted and kissed the top of her head.

Hazel giggled. "Yes, kissing you if we were together." She sat up and frowned. "How are we going to make this work? We live hours apart."

Nelson gave her an indulgent grin. "I know it might be hard to remember because I'm so awesome otherwise, but I *am* a billionaire. We actually own a plane, if neither of us want to drive the three hours to see each other."

Hazel closed her eyes and laughed, then leaned her forehead against his. "Got it. So, we're going to make this work, huh?"

"I sure hope so," he said. "I'm game if you are."

"Well, I already did write us a happy ending. We might as well make it come true."

"Absolutely," Nelson agreed as he pulled her in to get it started.

EPILOGUE

Once again, Hazel found herself in a position where she felt like she might hyperventilate. *How do I let him talk me into these things? Oh yeah, it's that handsome face of his.*

Nelson pulled the large goggles down over his eyes, his smile so wide it nearly split his face. "Ready?" he shouted over the drone of the airplane.

"No!" she shouted back.

Nelson laughed and gave her a thumbs up.

The guide strapped to Hazel's back chuckled and put his own thumb up as well.

Hazel and Nelson had been dating for six months and it had been the most glorious time of Hazel's life. Not a single week had gone by that they hadn't visited each other. Because Hazel could work from anywhere, she often came up and spent several days at the resort. The family had allowed her to stay in Cadence's old cabin and Hazel would write during the day, while Nelson did his activities. Then they would spend their evenings and weekends together.

Nelson had travelled down to meet her family and everyone had loved his friendly and outgoing personality. *He had fit right in,* Hazel thought wryly.

She grinned as she watched Nelson roll his neck and shoulders, then bounce on his toes as he prepared for the moment in front of them.

The grin dropped in an instant when a man standing next to Nelson put his hand to his ear set, then shouted. "Here we go!" With the push of a button, a door in the side of the plane opened.

"Oh my gosh, oh my gosh, oh my gosh," Hazel said quickly. *Never again. Never again will I allow his cute grin and fantastic kisses to sway me from my common sense.* Even as she thought the words, she knew they were useless. All he had to do was pull her close, and she melted, putty to his every whim.

"Here we go, Babe!" Nelson smiled and jumped, disappearing from view.

Hazel gasped. "Nelson!"

"Let's join him!" The guide behind her walked forward, forcing Hazel's legs into action.

"Um... I think maybe- AHHHH!" Hazel put her hands over her eyes as her body was forcibly shoved out of the plane and she and her instructor took to the air. She screamed until she ran out of air, but the wind rushing at her face made it difficult to get another good lungful.

Jason, her instructor, tapped her arm.

Hazel shook her head, and she felt him chuckle once again.

Jason tapped harder this time and Hazel pushed him away. "Hazel!" he shouted over the roar of the wind. "You really want to see this!"

Nelson has always taken care of me. I will be fine. This will be fine. Clenching every muscle in her body, Hazel forced her hands away from her goggles. At first, she couldn't see much, the scenery blurred together, but slowly, she began to make out the shapes of small objects beneath them. *Whoa...*

An arm was thrust into her line of vision and Hazel followed it to see Jason pointing at something. Following the tip of his finger, Hazel found Nelson falling not too far in front of them. His arms and legs were spread wide and that crazy smile still adorned his face.

He nodded his head and suddenly Hazel felt a hard jerk as their parachute deployed and slowed their progress. As she caught her breath from the sudden change, she looked at the man she loved again and promptly forgot to breathe.

As he floated lazily toward the earth, Nelson held a sign in front of him. It flapped in the breeze, but the writing was clearly legible.

WILL YOU MARRY ME?

Hazel put her hands over her mouth and felt tears prick her eyes. For a moment she couldn't move. Her heart felt like it would beat out of her chest and her vision was blurry.

The smile on Nelson's face began to droop and Hazel knew she had waited too long. Dropping her hands, she let him see her wide smile and nodded her head vigorously. "Yes," she said, even knowing he couldn't hear her. "Yes, I'll marry you."

Nelson dropped the sign and gave a whoop, punching a fist in the air.

Hazel laughed and whooped back. For the next several minutes, Hazel couldn't take her eyes from her fiancé. All the beauty around her and the adrenaline rush of the jump paled in comparison to knowing he was going to be hers forever.

Their landing couldn't come fast enough and Hazel was clumsier than usual as she and Jason dropped into the open field.

"Hang tight," Jason muttered as he helped her climb out of all the gear. Once free, she took off running in the direction Nelson had landed.

Nelson climbed out of his own gear and stepped clear of the chute. Opening his arms, he waited for Hazel to reach him and nearly fell to the ground when she slammed into his body.

"I love you, I love you, I love you!" she said over and over again, gripping him tightly.

Nelson kissed the top of her head. "I love you, too. More than you'll ever know." Putting his hands on both sides of her head, Nelson pulled her back so he could look into her eyes. "You complete me, Hazel. You believe in me and you trust me in a way that I've never experienced before. You make me want to be the hero you wrote me to be." He kissed her nose. "I think it's time to start a new story, hmm?"

Hazel's eyes were closed as she nodded her agreement.

"Perfect," Nelson murmured against her lips. "Let's get started now." No more words were said for a very... long... time.

SIGH

These two were some of my favorites!
This story makes me want to curl up with
a blanket and chocolate and not
emerge until I'm done. :)
Not ready to be done with the romance yet?
No worries! Teagan's story is next in
"Her Billionaire Gardener".